ALL MOST

D1738957

ALL MOST

Maryann D'Agincourt

PP
Portmay Press
New York

"Autumn Whorl" first appeared in *Able Muse*. "Desires" first appeared in *Italian Americana*. "Equity" first appeared in *The Iconoclast*.

Cover design by Patricia Fabricant

Cover image © 2013 Museum of Fine Arts, Boston. Oskar Kokoschka, Austrian, 1886–1980. *Two Nudes (Lovers)*, 1913, oil on canvas, 163.2 x 97.5 cm (64 1/4 x 38 3/8 in.), Museum of Fine Arts, Boston. Bequest of Sarah Reed Platt, 1973.196

Printed in the United States of America
First printing, 2013

Publisher's Cataloging-in-Publication
(Provided by Quality Books, Inc.)
D'Agincourt, Maryann.
     All most / Maryann D'Agincourt.
     pages cm
     ISBN 978-0-9891745-8-9 (hc)
     ISBN 978-0-9891745-3-4 (pb)
     ISBN 978-0-9891745-4-1 (e-book)
1. Short stories.   I. Title.
PS3604.A3325A45 2013   813'.6
                   QBI13-600147

Portmay Press
244 Madison Avenue
New York, NY 10016
www.portmaypress.com

Also by Maryann D'Agincourt

Journal of Eva Morelli
Glimpses of Gauguin
Printz
Shade and Light

For Nick

With special thanks to Emily Albarillo

A memory is a beautiful thing, it's almost a desire that you miss.
—*Gustave Flaubert*

Contents

ALL MOST

Dry air hissed from the floor vent as I pushed open the heavy glass door, leaving the hotel with a sudden rush of sadness. It was late August, the summer heat lingering like the scent of pine long after a fire's gone out. Yet there was a bluish gleam in the early evening sky, the first hint of autumn. I dropped my suitcase onto the pavement, and as cars zoomed by I searched up and down René Lévesque for a taxi. The glare of lights from the automobiles blurred my vision.

Out of the corner of my eye I saw the doorman coming toward me, his cheeks sunken, his shoulders narrow. He raised his hand as if he were about to wave, asking if I needed a cab to the airport. When I nodded, he picked up my suitcase and I followed him to a waiting car. As he put my luggage into the trunk, I went to open the door, but realized there was someone inside. I turned to the doorman and he explained there was a shortage of taxis. I'd have to share one if I needed to get to the airport soon. He touched my arm, his face solemn, and said it would save me money. Then, somberly, he winked.

When I got in, I glanced at the other passenger, a man in his late twenties, attractive in a robust sort of way, heavy, smiling lips, a prominent chin. As the taxi sped away, I turned to wave to the doorman, who had not moved from the curb.

During the ride to the airport, we didn't speak; instead we gazed out opposing windows. I watched the passing city, the summer night darkening, and noticed those walking home slouching, perhaps after a long day at work.

My thoughts drifted to my last trip to Montreal, two years before, with my husband, the same hotel. And at that moment I realized I'd forgotten to leave my key at the front desk and was still clutching it in my hand. Tightly grasping it, I remembered how he'd usually forget his hotel key, leaving it in the room. And again I felt that same sense of sadness. He was in his late fifties, and his illness had been sudden and brief. Though when I married him I had accepted that I'd probably outlive him, I never imagined losing him before I reached thirty-nine.

I'd met him when I was an intern at a New York newspaper with a modest circulation, where he was the film critic. It was the summer before my senior year of college.

On the last day of class that spring I had learned that I'd been accepted into the internship program. The person I would be replacing had decided instead to go to Europe for the summer, and I was next on the list. An only child, I was more eager to go to New York than to pursue a career in journalism. I'd grown up in a suburb of Philadelphia and attended college not far from my family home. The chance to get away from my overly protective parents was tantalizing. But I soon discovered how lonely it could be in New York, and by early July I was longing for summer to end.

My first contact with my future husband was during lunch break the day after the Independence Day holiday. He was walking toward the office building as I was about to leave. I vaguely recognized him as someone who worked in the office. He carried a paper bag in his hand and it occurred to me that he must eat alone at his desk. He was tall and slender, and wore a bow tie. His eyes were deep set and his forehead was flat. Without looking at me, he held the door open, and I slipped out of the building, not looking back.

I began to work late. Staying on until eight or nine in the evening helped curb my loneliness. And on most nights he'd linger in the office as well, and would still be working when I left.

Cautiously, I began to inquire about him. When I spoke to an assistant of his, I pretended to be critical of his intensity, how aloof he seemed, and said that I thought he was married to his work. His assistant shrugged, and then nodded. I discovered he had indeed never married and his family consisted of his parents, one brother, and one sister, all living in the Midwest.

One night we were the only two remaining in the office. As I struggled to edit an article my mentor had given me to work on, a piece about a children's summer theater group, he came over to my desk.

I believe he stood there for about ten minutes before I noticed him. When I looked up, the first thing I saw was his bow tie, and then his smile, his deeply etched dimples conveying both optimism and caution.

Later that evening he was surprised when I told him my age. It was a soft summer night, and the sprinkling of lights that remained on in the office buildings around us were like low-lying stars. As we strolled down Fifth Avenue, I noticed how he walked in a loose way, as if he were on a country road instead of a sidewalk in midtown Manhattan.

~

Breathless after climbing the four steep flights of stairs to his apartment, I stood behind him on the top step, careful not to look down as he unlocked the door.

Inside, videos filled the shelves of a mahogany bookcase that covered one wall of his living room. The apartment was small, crowded, still. And I thought how lonely he must be.

He asked if I'd like some wine. As he poured a glass for each of us, he announced that there was a French movie he wanted me to see—his favorite. But when he sat beside me on the sofa, I put my glass on the coffee table, next to his, and then reached out to him. For not only was I lonely, but I longed to care for him, to protect him. At first he seemed startled, but he soon accepted my caresses, my kisses, and hesitantly returned them in kind.

He insisted on bringing me home, and refused to stay the night with me. After he left, I went to look out the window. There was no trace of him. And I imagined him walking in that loose way of his back to his apartment, chiding himself, I believed, for becoming involved with someone so young.

I never saw that French movie, nor can I remember the name of it. But if I heard it, I would know.

He began to tutor me in writing. The following Monday, after the others had left the office for the day, he came over to my desk. Folding his arms, swaying a little, he asked if I thought I might like to become a film critic.

Awed, I looked up at him, thinking of what had happened between us a few nights before. Then he sat on my desk, crossed his ankles, and said the best movie reviews are full and alive, but not too long, never too long. "When you write about a film, Mona, you must be dispassionate," he said, "whether you are enthralled by it or detest it. You need to rein in your enthusiasm." And then he caught my gaze, his eyes concerned, and said, "Reining in—that is the most difficult part."

And he had been right; it was not easy for me to write in a controlled way. I lacked an unbiased eye. But he was an unrelenting teacher, and I was a diligent student.

Under his tutelage I soon became adept at writing reviews. On most nights we'd sit in his living room and watch an old movie. From time to time he'd stop the film and turn to me with a concentrated expression, asking me pointed questions. Then he'd explain various camera angles, and each actor's strengths and weaknesses.

I succumbed to his ardor for film, and with his help my reviews were soon published.

As the taxi pulled up to the airport terminal, my thoughts shifted to the present. Once the driver stopped the car and announced the airline, we got out through separate doors. He took our luggage from the trunk, and we each paid him.

It had grown dark, and I saw that my taxi companion was hesitant, didn't seem to be heading in any particular direction. Clutching my suitcase, I looked directly at him and asked if he needed help. He was about three inches taller than I was. I took in his gleaming eyes, his open expression. His form was strong and wiry, and for a moment I felt off-kilter just looking at him, addressing him.

He said it was his first time in the Montreal airport as he had taken the train in from New York. And as we walked into the terminal, he told me he was flying to New York now, but the next morning he'd fly home.

"Home, where is home?" I asked, perhaps sounding too inquisitive.

"The West Coast—San Francisco," he answered with a broad smile, his brows raised. Nothing hidden about him, I perceived, feeling uneasy.

We soon realized we were on the same flight. And as we went through security, I felt his presence behind me, like a shadow. Once we got to the gate, it was announced that because of the weather in New York our flight would be delayed. Thunderstorms, I assumed.

We sat down next to each another in plastic chairs in the waiting area. After five minutes or so he asked if I'd like a cup of coffee, and I suggested we go to the nearby restaurant instead, as it was closer than the coffee shop. I was concerned because I had promised the babysitter who was looking after my three-year-old daughter that I'd be in before midnight.

Again he smiled in an expressive way and nodded. We went into the restaurant, sat down, and ordered drinks.

There was silence and I was too anxious to talk, worrying about my daughter, not liking the idea of flying into the city in the aftermath of a thunderstorm, and then there was him, his presence, open and earnest.

He broke the silence, asking if I had gone to Montreal on business.

"Yes," I said. "I went to the film festival—I am a film critic. It's the first time I've been alone in this city. My husband was also a film critic, but he died about ten months ago. It was my first time back without him." I attempted to speak matter-of-factly. Ever since my husband had passed away, I had trained myself to do so. I knew I must be strong and accept his death. But it wasn't always easy, and as I was suddenly feeling scattered, my words might not have sounded as I'd hoped.

Emotion covered his face. "Your loss is a tragic one. He must have been young."

When I told him my husband's age, he shrugged and said that was young. He looked away, out the window, seeming to study an airplane slowly pulling away from a gate. When he turned back to look at me, he appeared pensive.

"What do you do?" I asked, holding my glass between the palms of my hands. "You are young, I think. Perhaps you haven't yet decided."

He smiled slightly, not answering my question.

He explained that he'd dabbled in different things, been a carpenter, sculpted some, and was now a . . . But just as he began to speak our flight was announced. We quickly left the payment for our drinks on the table and hurried toward the gate.

Our seats were at opposite ends of the plane. During the short flight back to New York, I took a quick nap, knowing I needed to rest before the frenzy of taking a cab from the airport to my apartment, paying the babysitter, and then the solace of holding my daughter in my arms, and rocking her to sleep.

As I was collecting my luggage from the conveyer belt after we had landed, I felt a tap on my shoulder. When I turned around, he was there, looking as friendly as he had all evening. Blushing, he handed me his card. And before I had a chance to tell him that it had been nice talking with him, he walked away without saying a word. I watched him wend his way through a crowd of people until I lost sight of him.

During the taxi ride home, I realized I was still holding the card he'd given me, but it was so dark I couldn't read it. There was a logo, but I couldn't make it out. I put the card in my jacket pocket and felt uplifted knowing I would soon see my daughter. Although I was tired, I longed to hold her, my Sophie, in my arms.

~

One month later, on a Saturday morning, I found his card in my linen jacket. It had grown cool and I was planning to bring my summer clothes to the cleaners that day. Sophie was still sleeping and I was rummaging through my closet, waiting for her to wake up. When I felt the card in the jacket pocket, I was surprised and sat down on the bed. As the crisp fall air flowed into the room, I lowered my eyes, remembering him. Then I raised the card; the light was bright and the card was easy to read. His name was Alexander Kane. The logo consisted of an A and a K placed in the center of the card, and a San Francisco address was listed beneath his name in the upper left hand corner. Apparently he was a writer and publisher of travel books.

Reflexively I positioned my hands to rip up the card, but at that moment Sophie came running into the room and jumped onto my lap.

Two weeks later I received a call from him. I was at my desk at work, finishing a review of a movie I had found slow and overly romanticized; I didn't want to offend the director, who had been a close friend of my husband's. Writing the article was a struggle because I wanted to be both tactful and honest. The ringing phone was a welcome diversion.

He asked me if I remembered him. Then I thought about the card he had given me, and wondered what I had done with it.

"Yes," I said. "Yes, I do remember you. How were you able to reach me?" I asked, knowing I had not given him my name.

"Your luggage tag—but it had your work address, not your home one, on it," he said, sounding as if he had enjoyed the challenge of tracking me down. Then he told me he was coming to New York in a week, and asked if I'd like to see him. As he spoke I looked out the window at the Halloween decorations on the storefront across the street and I smiled, thinking how it was only the middle of October. Too early, I thought. He seemed to sense my distraction as he repeated his question. "Yes," I said, assuredly. "Yes, I would like to see you."

The following weekend we met for lunch at an Italian restaurant on Ninth Avenue. It was a windy day. I got there first, went inside, and was escorted to a table. When I sat down I pressed my hands against my cold cheeks. And from the front window, I saw him walk hurriedly down the street toward me. His expression sharp and his eyebrows raised, seemingly focused on his destination, oblivious of the strong drafts.

I kept my eyes on him, watched him come into the restaurant, hastily look around, lower his head to speak to the host, and then follow the host to my table.

When I stood up to greet him, he warmly and firmly grasped my arms as if we were old friends or lovers, and I remembered how he said he'd been a carpenter for a few years, and even had sculpted some.

Later, after a long lunch and two bottles of wine, we sat naked on the bed in his hotel room. I clutched the sheet, tears streaming down my face, believing my intimacy with Alex, a stranger, had defiled my marriage. Not only was my husband dead, but so was any memory that remained of our sexual life together. My body shook and I began to sob. Alex had not encouraged me to drink the wine, nor had he seduced me—I had come to the hotel with him willingly, desirously.

He remained silent. After a while he got up and began to pace, his face reddening, his feet sweeping across the carpet. Then he came over, lay next to me, stroked the back of my ear, and began to hum what sounded like a lullaby. I turned my gaze toward the window, and through my tears I saw that dusk was setting in.

Eventually I stopped crying. I was empty. I had not cried with so much abandon in two years, not since I'd found out about my husband's illness.

When I looked over at Alex, I saw that his eyes were misty. My heart pounding, I reached out to him, pressing my mouth again and again to his body, then wrapped myself around him, not wanting to let him go.

Although we lived on separate coasts, our relationship soon became all consuming. He'd often come to New York, or I'd meet him in France or Italy. And he'd take me to the most unusual places, cities and towns unfamiliar to me—Avoriaz in the French Alps, Taranto in southern Italy.

I became so obsessed with our relationship that I'd repeatedly check my watch if he didn't call when he said he would, even if he was only two or three minutes late. While speaking with a colleague, I'd picture Alex's ardent expression, then I'd lose my train of thought. Yes, I, who had never been distracted by anything, let alone passion, had become terribly unfocused.

In May I took a leave of absence from my work, left Sophie with my parents in Pennsylvania, and joined Alex in San Francisco for the summer.

Although he worked mostly from his apartment, I'd miss him if he went out to do an errand. I'd even miss him while he was working in the next room. But I never doubted that he was more interested in me than in his work.

From his apartment we could see the bay. Often we'd stay up all night, never speaking very much, just sitting out on the porch, looking out into the distance at the twinkling lights, each holding a glass of wine, our bodies spent.

Twice that summer I went to visit Sophie, and the second time Alex came with me. She seemed surprised to see him, and either cried or was cranky for most of the visit. My father was away on a golf trip with his friends. While Alex was respectful to her, my mother didn't reveal to me what she thought of him. Yet I could feel his eyes on me at all times. It was as if my presence was what sustained him.

During the entire plane ride back to San Francisco, my eyes were filled with tears. He didn't say anything, he simply watched me, his face expressing concern, but not guilt, never guilt.

When we returned to his apartment late that night, we did not make love. He cradled my head in his arms, his way of lulling me to sleep. He didn't say anything, he simply looked off into the distance, a breeze coming in from the open window and ruffling the strands of hair that had fallen across his forehead. I'd never felt his love for me more.

I was drawn to him because I meant so much to him, because he longed for me. And as obsessed as I was with him, with our physical relationship, I began to wonder if my need for him did not equal his for me, if his was more emotional. After all, I had a child. Although I had left Sophie with my parents for the summer, not one day passed that I didn't think of her, didn't yearn for her presence. There were days when I'd call her two or three times. Sometimes she'd be thrilled to hear my voice, and at other times she'd not want to talk at all. I began to feel uneasy and wonder how I would feel when I returned to New York in September, to my work, and to Sophie. For it was becoming more and more clear that my city, my reviews, and my daughter were what grounded me.

In late July, Alex and I went to France. He needed to update his travel book on Paris. All of his books were small, pocket-sized. Each day he'd choose a different arrondissement, and we'd spend hours walking through it. As his attention was mostly on me, I never saw him take notes. But from time to time he'd glance about, notice something he had not before seen. He'd investigate whatever it was—a restaurant, a statue, a new hotel or art gallery—and I suspected it would appear in the updated book.

In his appreciation of place he was artistic. He wasn't, as is often the case with travel writers, factual in a painstaking way. To the contrary, he wrote about his impressions. Every city, every hotel, every restaurant, every work of art he liked he took to heart, as if he were the one who had found the city, built the hotel, prepared the food in a restaurant, or painted the painting in a museum. He did so not because he was egotistical, but because he was exuberant as well as inherently naïve.

Our last night in Paris we had dinner at a small restaurant on the Boulevard St. Germain. It was an exceedingly warm night and though we would be together for at least another month, I sensed our impending separation. But Alex was in a fine mood. He had dressed up for dinner, wearing a narrow tie and linen jacket. His hair, normally unkempt, was combed to the side.

He smiled readily, appearing more content and relaxed than usual; our passion for each other often made him pensive, overly serious.

Over dinner, he didn't look at me; he seemed to concentrate on his food, first mussels and then a rack of lamb. That night as he dexterously opened the mussels, I watched his hands intently, appreciating his ease. I was surprised, as he'd never been very graceful when eating.

When we finished our meal, he took my hand and told me he'd come to Paris as a child with his parents and had wandered away from them in the Louvre. Realizing he was lost, he had gone up to one of the museum guards, who spoke enough

English to understand that he could not find his parents. The guard had comforted him, making strange faces so that he would laugh. Alex said he had been so diverted by this man that he'd almost forgotten he was lost. But when his parents found him, they were angry, very angry. And, he said, they never really trusted him after that. That distrust became a habit for them and it continued on into his adult life. Yes, there were other instances when they hadn't approved of something he'd done—all minor things—but that reflexive distrust had started then, that time in Paris. Then he glanced around the restaurant as if he didn't want anyone to hear what he was about to say. When he looked back at me, he told me that he had decided to move to New York, and would be there by mid-October.

I was startled by the news. Though my time with him had been healing, I realized at that moment how much I still grieved for my husband.

As fond of and as deeply attracted as I was to Alex, I did not know if I loved him. Over the past two years, I had lost my sense of love. I loved my daughter—maternal love was the only love I could now comprehend.

The lights along the boulevard glowed as I looked out the restaurant window. Then I turned to him and said, "I don't know. My husband was alive not so very long ago. I don't know. Part of me believes he will return, he will come home. But a greater part of me knows I have lost him forever."

He half smiled and said, "Don't worry. I understand. I am coming to New York. It is settled. We do not need to live together. I have already found a place."

As he spoke, I felt crushed, deflated by his emotional certainty. Yet my passion for him had never been more vibrant.

~

That last month in San Francisco was both painful and exhilarating. We'd sit for hours at a bar on the top floor of a hotel, gazing out the window, as if we were flying over the city, watching the sky darken over Alcatraz.

Then when we returned to his apartment, we'd throw ourselves together as if we'd never before experienced joy or intimacy.

One morning at breakfast, about a week before I would be returning to New York, he looked at me, his eyes sad but fiery, and said that it would be difficult for him to not see me for a month, that it would be a long September for him. He needed me to stay with him.

Though his expression was beseeching, he spoke fervently—it was as if he had tied me in a chair with his passion, his desire. And I became agitated.

Before I knew it he lifted me in his arms and carried me out onto the porch, sat me on the wall. But when I turned to him, he had already gone back inside. I sat out there alone, not knowing what to do. I could only think of Sophie and my work. If I lost them, I would lose myself.

When he brought me to the airport one week later, we said very little to each other. I knew he loved me too much to intrude on what I most wanted, and that was to be able to live for my daughter and my work.

My mother and Sophie were already at the apartment when I arrived. They had flown in from Philadelphia a day earlier. I stood in the doorway and watched Sophie closely; she was exploring the living room, standing on the sofa, touching the books on the shelves, while my mother sat close to her.

When Sophie turned to look at me she was at first startled, then she seemed shy. I went up to her and caressed her hair with my hand, tears in my eyes, happy to be home.

My mother rose from the sofa and embraced me. "You needed this time away, Mona—good for you." And it reminded me of how she had said, "Good for you," when in high school instead of going to my best friend's first flute performance with a young-adult orchestra, I had gone out on a date with a boy I'd just met and would never see again.

"I missed Sophie," I said. "I missed her terribly." And as I looked at my daughter, for a brief moment I saw my husband's expression in her darting eyes.

Sophie watched as I unpacked in my bedroom. Joyfully she bounced up and down on the mattress as if it were a trampoline. It must have struck her that she was home and so was I, and we wouldn't be leaving.

"Look," I said, "Look what I have for you!" And as I dangled a toy Golden Gate Bridge before her, she came and wrapped her arms around me. I lost my balance and the toy fell from my hand.

"Where is it?" she cried out. "Where is it?" On her knees, she scoured the floor, and I did so as well. I put my hand beneath the bed and felt something. I knew it wasn't the toy, but I pulled it out. It was Alex's card, the one he'd given me that night at the airport when I first met him. It was a little bent and soiled, and there was a slight tear in it. I held on to it, not able to let it go. Despite Sophie's cries, her wanting to take it from me, I clutched it more and more tightly.

From time to time I would call Alex. And every month or so we'd meet for a drink, but nothing more. He was pleased that he had moved to New York. But the last time I saw him he told me he was giving up the travel-writing business—he'd never thought he was that good at it. The small inheritance he had received from his grandfather that had been subsidizing was nearly spent. Instead, he was planning to go to Haiti to help build a school. He was a pretty solid carpenter, he said, and thought he could help out. Maybe he'd start to sculpt again.

When we said good-bye, he didn't kiss me, or even touch me; he just looked at me in that heartfelt way of his and walked away without waving. Were there tears in my eyes? His? I don't remember.

As emotionally hesitant as my husband had been, Alex, to the contrary, had been effusive, uninhibited. And though I had relished my time with Alex, I knew I could not live the sort of life he desired. For I had learned early and from an expert teacher to rein in passion.

Yet the question remains: Did I love him? Almost.

Autumn Whorl

In the afternoon sun, fallen leaves moist from a soft morning rainfall were strewn across the sidewalk like embers. It was a breezy October day. On my way home from school, pressing my homework folder to my chest to protect the sheets inside from the wind, I half wondered if my mother would be home. Because of his work the past few months, my father had to be in New York on weekdays. In his absence it was as if our house suddenly had a large hole in the center and my mother and I both had to walk gingerly around its periphery. We were surprised, as we hadn't realized how much of a part he played in holding the three of us together. So we occupied ourselves with other things, things that led us away from that dark, unseen hole.

Mother enrolled in a course in art history at the museum, a seminar on Rembrandt, and said she would apply for graduate credit. She studied more now, and I'd often find her in the middle of the night in the small study at the back of our home, wrapped in her green velvet bathrobe, hunched over the typewriter, punching the keys. She'd be sleepy but determined, a half-filled cup of tea rattling on her desk. I'd stand behind her and watch. She wouldn't turn her head; she'd just keep typing. After a while she'd stop, then lift her chin. Clacking a red-painted fingernail against one key, she'd say, "Jocelyn, honey, it's time now to go to bed." I'd tiptoe out of the room, and she wouldn't resume typing until I was halfway down the hall. My mother put her whole self into writing. When she held one of the papers she'd been working on in her hand, it was as if it was a part of her body, another limb.

Lately I'd begun to see a change in her; she was less critical than when my father was at home, less questioning of my whereabouts, but at the same time she was more affectionate toward me, more so than she'd been in the past.

Because she'd been spending more and more time at the library and wasn't certain how long she'd need to study on a particular day, she'd given me a key to let myself in. When I reached the house that day, I rang the bell and waited. She wasn't home. I pulled out the key from my skirt pocket and opened the door. Soon I went into the study to do to my homework. I found Mother's papers scattered across the top of the desk. Because the blinds of the single window that faced the backyard were closed, the title of the paper was difficult to read.

I had a math assignment, some word problems to work on, and I needed more light to see the numbers on the sheet. Before I sat down, I put my mother's papers in the top drawer of the desk and then pulled open the venetian blinds. The strong autumn light filled the room. From where I stood I could see the entire backyard—and there under the maple tree sat my mother, among the deep-red leaves on the ground. Her ankles and feet were hidden beneath her dark green billowy skirt; the buttons on her burgundy blouse were undone. At that moment a strong breeze blew, opening her shirt, fully revealing her small breasts. I stuck my fist inside my mouth to prevent myself from crying out—she was not alone. My art teacher, wearing the same gray pants and white shirt he'd had on in class that day, stood a few feet away from her holding a large pad of paper in one hand with a low-burning cigarette between two fingers. His other hand moved quickly across the sheet. He sketched freely, unmoved by the sight of my mother's breasts. With his head lowered to the paper in concentration, his expression was earnest, absorbed, his dark shiny hair falling across his forehead. I yanked the window cord with my free hand and the blinds snapped shut. Then I ran upstairs to my bedroom, locked the door, and got into bed and under the covers. As I lay there I kept replaying in my mind my mother's calm, steady expression, her small breasts, the art teacher's impartial, sweeping glance, the quick movement of his hand as he sketched. And at that moment I wished the maple tree had not been so close, so easy to see from where I stood. It was as if I was looking through binoculars, and my mother and he were unnaturally close to me, every detail of their beings exposed, enlarged by the strong lenses. Though my mind was racing and my heart thumping beyond control, I remained quiet and still beneath the covers, fearful that any movement on my part would draw attention to my whereabouts.

Soon I heard the back door open, and then the sound of their footsteps in the kitchen, their voices low, weary sounding. I blocked my ears; I didn't want to listen to their words. I lay in bed with my eyes tightly closed, imagined my mother insisting that he stay, her expression pleading, her hair falling down past her shoulders, her blouse open. I pressed my hands even more firmly against my ears and held still in this position, yearning to roll in the leaves.

EQUITY

Reading from her notes, my sister, Linette, says in her quiet, exacting way, "The second child is usually flexible, willing to cooperate."

The approaching steps of our waitress distract me for a moment. The waitress, in an ankle-length satin dress, pours water into each of our glasses, and then shuffles away.

Linette is a freelance writer. This month she's been assigned to write an article about birth order for a psychology magazine, with an emphasis on the second child. Although she needs to interview a number of second children, she wants to begin with me; she believes I am the perfect second child. Linette's concern with specificity—it is as if she puts each of her interactions into a box with a label—often makes me uncomfortable. Her "labeling technique" is what I like to call this proclivity of hers, and I believe she uses it as a means of discourse to distance herself from me, her younger sister.

It is a cold mid-April afternoon and whenever the door of the restaurant opens, there is a sudden draft around my knees. My skirt today is shorter than usual; my legs are exposed. This morning, I became conscious of this when Jack, my boss, strolled over to my desk to hand me some letters he wanted typed.

Jack wasn't really busy, just catching up on some personal correspondence. He's never learned to type and looks awkward when he does it using one finger on his laptop. "It's like having a learning disability," he says in his self-deprecating way, whenever he needs me to type personal correspondence for him.

"I apologize for asking you to type letters—I'm not quite certain it is in your job description." He handed me the work, and out of the corner of my eye, I saw him look at me with that hungry expression of his. I ignored him, concentrating on the screen.

"You are very much the model second child. You're not competitive—although you have a college degree, you are working as an administrative assistant, and this doesn't bother you," Linette says. Then, hastily, she adds, "Naturally, everyone is an individual, with his her own biases, proclivities—so nothing I say is the absolute truth. It has nothing to do with truth, it has to do with degree—personal choice." She speaks emphatically, her cheeks reddening.

I focus on her small pointed face, as if reading on it tiny, nearly indecipherable print, while I silently ponder Jack and his wife, their marriage. Jack's wife is English; they've been married for three years, no children. When I began to work for him six months ago, Jack confided in me, told me his wife was having trouble adjusting to American life. The more I know him the more I believe it is Jack she is having difficulty adjusting to, not American life. He is somewhat chameleon-like. When he is with a client, he appears composed, his fine white-blond hair in place, his tie carefully knotted, his tone gentle, and he is organized in the presentation of his work. On days when he's not with a client, papers are strewn across his desk, his tone is blunt, his shirt is wrinkled, his posture slumped.

The only time Jack directly approached me was when we were riding alone in an elevator one early December evening, after work. We were the last ones to leave the office that day. As we passed the ninth and then the eighth floor, he glanced at me, then suddenly he put his arm around my waist, kissed me hard, wet on the mouth, his briefcase bumping my legs. He kissed me until the lobby bell sounded. As the elevator door opened he said in a direct and passionate voice, "Jessica, I'll never touch you again unless you want me to." When I saw Jack the next day at work, I pretended it hadn't happened, avoiding his gaze as I have been doing these past four months.

I am attracted to him—I understand and like his more often than not rumpled appearance, his self-deprecating wit, his bluntness. But before anything more happens between us, I need to know what it is he wants—sex, to hurt his wife, or love. After all this time, I'm still not certain.

A month ago, Linette asked me in that insistent way of hers if I was having an affair with a married man.

Looking down at her, eyeing her glassy, wavering irises, I said, "Why do you ask?" We were in the lobby of a movie theater, waiting for the usher to let us in to see the film.

"You seem preoccupied lately, uneasy. Take care of yourself, Jessica." That was all she said, then she crossed her arms and walked toward the food counter to buy some popcorn.

I was surprised Linette had asked me a question related to sex; we had never before discussed that aspect of relationships, as she is not a physical sort of person. I suspect that, at twenty-six, she is sexually inexperienced.

I study her across the table; she is sipping water from her

glass, the lemon wedge bumping her tiny nose, her expression earnest. She suddenly appears vulnerable. And I think of elementary school, how I would defend her on the playground when other children teased her. I looked older than Linette and was taller and stronger than she was. She would stand meekly next to me, clutching a book in one hand, her shoulders hunched, as other children taunted her because she didn't want to participate in the kickball game.

She was a straight-A student. I, on the other hand, was a competent athlete, but in terms of schoolwork, I tended to put things off and do my homework at the last possible moment.

From as far back as I can remember, our parents appreciated how different we were. While delighting in Linette's academic skills, they always praised me for what they call my strong sense of responsibility. I was the one who organized the household chores once Mother decided to return to work. And now I can afford to rent my own apartment, while Linette still lives at home with our parents. Administrative assistants earn more money than freelance writers.

Linette now speaks about the second child and relationships, how sometimes the second child can be impulsive, not fully considering the consequences of his or her actions. I imagine Jack kissing me in his office, my back pressed against the locked door, and I feel the same tingly, expectant sensation I had when he kissed me in the elevator.

Linette asks if I am okay. What she really wants to know is whether or not I am paying close attention to what she's saying.

"I'm fine," I assure her.

"Jessica," she says, sounding very serious. "Working on this article has inspired me. I've decided to make a career change. I'd like to study psychology, perhaps earn a doctorate in the field."

"Why not?" I answer, thinking about the expense.

Our parents had informed us before Linette started college that they could afford only half of our undergraduate tuitions at a state university. Linette has already spent her half.

"Do you think it will interfere with my life?" Linette asks. For a moment she appears anxious, wistful. I know she is referring to her personal life, an emotional relationship that is presently nonexistent.

"If it is important to you, Linette, you must do it," I say.

Beaming confidently now, she reaches across the table, past the empty dishes and water glasses, and squeezes my hand. I realize how much Linette respects me; I feel warmly accepted.

"I know somehow you'll manage to pay for this degree," I say with much goodwill toward her. Again she reaches across the table for my hand, her cheeks glowing. But her touch is cold this time.

"Mom and Dad have offered to help by taking out a loan," she says quickly, as if she has practiced this line many times over. "They thought, to be fair, I should tell you; ask for your blessing."

"But I haven't asked our parents for help since college, and I don't believe I ever will again," I say decisively.

"Exactly," Linette answers.

"Oh," I say, releasing my hand from hers. I check my watch. "Sorry, my lunch hour is up. Jack will be angry if I am a minute late."

I avoid her surprised gaze and drop a twenty-dollar bill onto the table.

"What about the interview?" she asks, her tone sharp, hassled.

As I shimmy out of the booth, I glance at her nonplussed expression, recalling how she'd stare in that same way when we were young, whenever I'd walk home from school with her, having just defended her on the playground. She'd never say a word. Just that same expression on her face, as if she were digesting and at the same time refuting what had happened to her.

"Another time," I answer, avoiding her gaze.

At the door, I turn to look at her one more time. She is still at the table, now assiduously writing in her notebook.

As I hurry to the office, to my computer, and to Jack, draft after draft of prickly April air strikes my face, a barrage of tiny, successive darts.

KIMONO

Blair Marinelli favored a pale, draping style of dress, reminiscent of that of a robed medieval scholar or a high-fashion model. But she was neither; she was a travel agent. And so tall that now, attempting to get a clear view of the city from her bedroom window, she thought it best to kneel. As she lowered her body, her knees brushed the soft carpeting and her elbows caught the sill.

Within moments it began to snow. Bright streetlights illuminated the swirling flakes falling slowly, gracefully, abundantly. It was as if all the stars in the universe were descending, she thought. And as whenever she witnessed beauty, Blair's eyes moistened. But once she stood up and turned away from the window, she could not hold on to this emotion; it was as if she had not experienced it. Instead, she felt a pulse of apprehension, as forceful as a charge of adrenaline. Her younger adopted brother, David, had called twenty minutes earlier to say he was coming to see her.

Since they'd never gotten along, she was uneasy in his presence. They had led different lives. But there were other reasons too—those nights when she was fifteen, and David thirteen; how he'd stealthily come into her bedroom and stand over her as she lay in bed. Just as he was about to pull off the blankets covering her bare breasts, she'd wake. "Go away," she'd say in a hostile, sleepy voice. And he'd leave, his head bent like a shamed puppy. After a month or so he never came again. In the morning she would not ask him why he had come to her room because she never knew if it really had happened, or if it had been a dream. But as an adult she knew that it had not been a dream.

Now, with a sense of determination, she grasped the gold knobs on the doors of her walk-in closet, opening them with aplomb. In the far corner a small bulb emitted a soft, dull light. As she pulled the kimono off the hanger, one narrow strap of her satin slip fell from her shoulder to her arm. She quickly turned her wrist and held the robe up to the faint light, the crepe-like material black, translucent. Her warm brown eyes were partially closed, her expression setting, like the sun lowering behind a veil of dark clouds.

She removed the kimono from her closet whenever she was in need of solace and assurance; at such times, like now, she tightly wrapped it around her tall, lean frame, humming a sharp note. She went into the kitchen, carefully put on a CD of *La Traviata*, and then set a kettle of water to boil for tea. As she sat on the wooden swivel stool at the breakfast bar, she remembered when she was child how Grandfather Marinelli would play a recording of a Verdi or Puccini opera on his old player. And while they listened to the music, Papa, as she'd called him, would explain, in a soft, accented voice, the story of Rigoletto or Madame Butterfly.

Blair's reverie was interrupted by the sound of the harsh, whistling kettle cutting into the fine opera, and her heart sank.

She had purchased the kimono when she'd been hired to

model nude for a college art class. An art professor had come up to her one fall day as she was walking across campus, and had asked her if she would like to earn some money. He was in his late fifties, his reputation strong as a teacher, straightforward as a person. He told her he needed a model for two of his classes, and she was the right height and form. He was having trouble finding someone. "If you don't want to do it, if it would make you uncomfortable or self-conscious, don't say yes," he had advised her.

But she had said yes, and that afternoon after her last class she had bought the kimono at a boutique across from the campus. She had been flattered to be noticed, and noticed in such a professional and objective way.

She had gone to the class early, before the others arrived. But when it came time for her to take off the kimono, she had been unable to disrobe. She had stood in front of the art class, peering at the waiting faces of the students standing before their easels. Abruptly, she had turned away, and had walked out of the room, her cheeks burning.

Now she had donned the kimono not only because David would be visiting but because it had become clear to her that she must shut down her shop, her travel shop as she liked to call it—her invention, so to speak. She had been ousted by internet travel. She was no longer needed, and would have to find a way to get out of her lease. It had gotten to this point because she'd never thought it would happen. She had refused to go online because she had always believed she possessed a sense of what was good and interesting and what was not, and she thought internet travel was not. Though sometimes she'd wonder if a universal rightness and truthfulness did not exist and it was simply her perceptions, personal, biased. At those times her life appeared very gray and uncertain, and she'd feel slightly deflated.

Now she experienced a creeping sense of fatigue as she realized she had seen it coming all along, but had never believed customers would not savor the romanticism of going to a travel agent, the mystery of their experience opening up before them. She had stuck to her perspective, and because of this she must look for other work, another way to promote travel. Though she had some time—she needed to work for reasons, and she acknowledged that they were not only financial: the satisfaction she received from watching customers coordinate their trips, their expressions at first anxious then smiling once they read the itinerary she had produced. Blair's gold charm bracelet, the only jewelry she wore, tinkled as she'd spread the computer printout before them. Her demeanor would remain impassive, though her spirits would lift, as she experienced a sense of gratitude, an affirmation of who she was—someone who represented pleasure, flight of the mind and body.

Despite this, she herself had never been a confident traveler; her hesitancy had prevented her from truly experiencing a different culture. It was the imagining part she had always liked best. What would have happened had she taken the tram to the highest point of Mont Blanc with the Austrian comedian she had met in a café one fine morning six or seven years ago? Instead, she had stood at the base of the great mountain and watched as the tram with the comedian inside climbed up until it was lost in the clouds. Or she'd envision herself someday, in the not-too-distant future, spending one night at the ice hotel in northern Finland, after years of longing to do so.

So with each customer she sought what she liked to call potential, the potential to experience what she had not been able to experience when traveling, the ability to roll up one's sleeves, to submerge oneself for a short period in another way of life, another culture, to attempt to speak the language, to relish the food. She'd see this potential in the sudden shift of a customer's eye, or a pointedly earnest expression, displaying restlessness, a need for something more.

Once, one of her customers, one of those she believed had this special ability, had called her when he returned from his trip through East Asia and had asked her out. He wanted to report to her, he had said jokingly. It was the beginning of an intense relationship that had lasted about six months. He had broken up with her because he said he had become too infatuated with her; he was suffocating.

Blair had been so angry after he left her that she had pounded her fist hard enough on the table to make the hanging lamp fall. It had cut her face, leaving a tiny scar beneath her left eye. This was the first and only time she had shown anger. What she had been most angry about was that she had always believed she was a free spirit, not controlling. He had undermined her sense of who she thought she was, what she represented. It had been crushing.

Now, in her bedroom, she placed the cup of tea on the bureau and stood in front of a full-length mirror assessing herself, her red hair bluntly cut above her shoulders, lightly brushing the kimono. She cringed at the thought of that experience. Slowly, she leaned forward, peering at her reflection in the mirror, touching the scar with her forefinger.

Stepping back from the mirror, she wrapped the belt of the robe tightly around her waist, grimacing at her reflection, as if to distance herself from the past, the unexplainable past.

The buzzer rang sharply and she turned to check the time on the digital clock next to her bed. It was eight thirty.

She walked quickly into the living room, the kimono flaring open, freeing her ankles. She pressed the button on the intercom, her ear against it to listen. She heard a hollow and static voice: "It's David."

Promptly, she pressed the button to unlock the front door.

When she first saw him, she smiled brightly, looked straight into his eyes; they were the same height. His body was erect, his hands thrust into his jacket pockets, his neck gliding forward, like an alert deer. His mushroom-colored eyes did not meet hers; they slid back and forth. It was a very cold January evening and Blair felt a draft coming from the hallway.

"Come in, David," she said, hearing impatience in her voice, yet at the same time knowing there was affection in it as well.

"That kimono, I remember it. It's worn a bit, but black suits you, your red hair. I remember it," he said again, fixing his gaze on the robe, removing one hand from his jacket pocket to point a finger at it.

Suddenly they heard a strong blast of wind coming from the balcony door, and together they walked toward it.

Crossing her arms, Blair watched David peer through the glass door onto the small balcony. The balcony was bare except for a small mound of old gray ice in the corner, almost blanketed by the newly fallen snow. He stood on tiptoe, raised his head, and looked out into the distance at the twinkling city lights.

"Great view, even with the snow," he said, as he turned toward her, one eyebrow raised. "I haven't been here in a while and I forget." She thought he sounded apologetic.

"What is it, David? Why are you here?" She now heard panic in her voice. Without waiting for his response, she moved toward the kitchen part of the living area. She glanced at him as she started to prepare coffee.

He did not answer her. Meticulously, he placed his jacket over the arm of a bulky leather chair, and then cautiously sat on the kitchen stool, the white breakfast bar between them. He smiled sheepishly.

"How's Anne?" she asked solicitously, tucking a strand of hair behind her ear.

"Busy," David said, quietly, bluntly. Blair poured coffee into the hot-pink ceramic mugs she had bought when she had last visited their parents in Florida.

Blair respected Anne because she knew Anne was devoted to her profession. She was a social worker. Anne's emotional reserve irritated Blair. She wasn't surprised David had married Anne. He had always been attracted to stoic women, women who camouflaged their feelings.

David wasn't happy. David would never have married someone who had allowed him to experience joy. He preferred living on the edge of unhappiness. He did love Anne, but in David's way of loving—at a distance, as if his wife were a work of art he admired. She could see this in the way he tilted his chin, the way his eyes narrowed when he spoke about her.

"I decided to close my business today," Blair announced.

"Why?"

"I have become obsolete," she said with a touch of irony in her voice.

"What will you do?"

"I don't know—I have never been so free."

She saw him look at her as if caught by her expression, and at that moment they connected.

"Where's Anne?" she asked, purposefully changing the subject.

"At a conference in Atlanta." He lifted his chin, looked directly at Blair. "Have you heard from our parents?" he asked. His eyes focused on her face, her expression. She felt confined, as if he was judging her in some way.

"They called last week. They do love the Florida weather. I can't believe it's been twelve years now; it seems as if they have been gone for only two or three. I don't worry about them. You know Mom is doing volunteer work now. She's a counselor for unwed teenage mothers; sixty-five years old, and she's found her niche."

David nodded. There was silence. Neither of them said what the other was thinking—how their mother was never an emotional presence in their lives. She was too involved in other people's lives, helping, supposedly. It was her way of coping with her husband's distant personality, his indirectness. And Frank, the oldest, was her favorite.

David swiveled around on his stool, away from Blair, to see out the balcony. She noticed his hunched shoulders. He seemed burdened, she thought. She longed to press him, to ask him about his marriage. After all these years, why weren't there any children? Was it a mutual decision? Was there something physically wrong? He'd been silent about this matter and so had Anne.

Blair knew David had been expecting to run their father's business someday, though he had never admitted this desire to his father. David had believed his father had understood his feelings, and was shocked when he sold the business to someone else.

Instead, David had accepted a job as a loan officer in a bank, and he'd been doing the same thing for ten years. How did he tolerate it? Blair wondered.

"I've been painting, Blair," David said out of the blue, swiveling around to stare directly at her.

"Houses?" Blair asked, incredulous, looking directly at him.

"No, people, some landscapes—mostly nudes," he said offhandedly.

As Blair attempted to hold David's gaze, his eyes shifted away, focusing on the coffee cup she was holding.

"I've been taking painting courses for the past few years, mostly oil painting. I don't know why I've never mentioned it to you before. My teacher said I have talent, for whatever that's worth. I can see myself moving in that direction. Anne's supportive."

"That's a change," Blair said, feeling angry, as if he were mocking her with this decision of his. But at that moment something compelled her to confront him. She wanted to make him uneasy. She looked directly at him and squinted. "Why, David?"

"It feels right, natural."

"Have you always done what is natural?" She heard a sharpness in her voice.

"Yes, I believe I have."

"Even when it wasn't right?" she asked, her heart now pounding.

He shrugged, blushing slightly.

Knowing that she had made her point, Blair thought of Mark, her friend for a number of years and her lover these past six months or so. Maybe they could take a vacation together while she decided what to do next with her life. She was happy with Mark. She didn't know how long it would last. She never knew. Sometimes a relationship would continue for a while, the happiness, the feeling of connectedness, and then suddenly it would be cut short over a minor argument or a change in plans and there was nothing left but a hardness, a distaste over what had been and for some unexplainable reason would never be as it was before.

"I'd better go," David said. And Blair knew she had conveyed to him her restlessness, her unease with him.

Her expression pensive, she pursed her lips and said, "Fine," as if she had just taken a long sip of a heavy, tart wine.

She walked David to the door, awkwardly put her arm through his. "Good luck with your art," she said, her expression wry, her voice low, willful. She squeezed his hand, the one he painted with, she believed. And just before he stepped out into the hallway, he turned and met her gaze. "Maybe one day I'll paint your portrait," he said wistfully.

"Maybe," she answered, not looking away.

Before calling Mark, she stepped in front of the full-length oval mirror in the bedroom. Her mouth was wide and her tilted nose seemed off center, as if she had just awakened from a nap, having slept wrong on a pillow. Her appearance reminded her of how she must have looked after she had escaped from being kissed by Henry when she was fourteen. She'd been told by her father that Henry, her grandparents' next-door neighbor, was not right in his mind, to not bother with him if she should see him outside in the yard. Upon hearing this, she had felt sorry for Henry; at the same time she had been compelled by him, by the way he stuttered when he spoke. One day he coaxed her in his bumbling way to go behind her grandfather's toolshed with him. It was a Sunday afternoon and the adults were inside her grandparents' house eating, conversing. She knew he was harmless, that she would be able to outsmart him if need be. As he tried to kiss her, she heard faint strands of music coming from the house, one of Verdi's operas playing over and over on her grandfather's outdated record player. Pushing him away, she imagined the sound of the scratchy needle she would hear when she was standing close to the record player—obsolete, but her grandfather had insisted on keeping it.

She had easily been able to free herself from Henry and had run towards the house, focusing on the yellow shutters. She shut her eyes and the music sounded stronger the closer she got to the house. She allowed the strains of the opera to inhabit her. When she opened the door and stood in the foyer, she was at a loss, feeling isolated from the conviviality surrounding her.

She now loosened the belt of her robe, shrugging herself out of the kimono, watching it gracefully drop to the floor and caress her ankles. She recalled music from *Madame Butterfly*. But she could not linger on that sad story, for at that moment she promised herself that no matter what, she would not allow herself to become a tragic figure. Ironic maybe, obsolete likely, but never tragic. Tightly closing her eyes so that she would be unable to see her naked reflection in the mirror, she wriggled out of the silk slip. The strains of "Un bel di, vedremo" that had been playing in her mind faded away. All she was aware of was how vigorously her heart pounded as, ever so slowly, she opened her eyes.

The Photograph

A dream, evocative, recurring, awakens Irina.

In the dream, she's on a white, sandy beach. It is a sunny, breezy day. Beside her is someone—but she is not certain of his or her identity; a face is hidden behind dark glasses, a baseball hat, raised knees. Suddenly it turns dark. Thunder. It is so dark she cannot see. How far is she from the ocean? Where is this person? She gropes and gropes, the sand wetting her fingers.

It is still night, and her face is wet with tears. She sits up in bed and looks out the window at the dark and empty street. When she clicks on the bedside light, her gaze meets the dusty, silver-framed photograph of her father propped up on the bureau. It was taken about a year before he left. The collar of his polo shirt turned up, he is smiling broadly, his eyes nearly closed, his face long, fine-boned. This photograph has become part of her; it is what she sees before she goes to bed each night and when she awakens the next day. Whenever she looks at it, she experiences a sense of solace yet when she stares at the smiling face for too long, she is uneasy.

Hours later she bathes in the winter morning darkness, her dream lingering in the back of her mind. Her thoughts are on her role in the new ballet, the very contemporary *Mauve*, as she dwells on what happens once the stage floor is flooded with light and the performance begins. Light—but now there is darkness. It is February and the natural light has been weak—no new-fallen snow to refract the natural gray cast. Already it is the third Saturday of the month. And with mixed feelings she remembers she has promised to spend the day with Jeremy.

It was spring, an evening in late April, ten months ago, when she met him. It was a blind date arranged by mutual friends, who thought they might connect—two Americans living in Montreal. As she crossed Crescent Street near the French restaurant where they had planned to meet, a light rain began to fall.

He stood next to the host in the candlelit foyer, and the black leather jacket he had mentioned he'd be wearing during their brief telephone conversation was shorter and tighter than she'd expected. His hair was a bit long in the back and she was surprised, because he'd said he was a businessman, had his own building company in Montreal. She had imagined him appearing more conservative, more precisely groomed. He looked away from her, toward the dining area. And with as much fortitude as she could muster, she went up to him and introduced herself.

Vividly she remembers his bemused expression, his restlessness that first evening over dinner as he told her that recently, inadvertently he'd discovered that his grandfather, his father's father, had been convicted of grand larceny! Theft! He'd found an old newspaper clipping pressed between the pages of his father's leather-bound copy of *The Brothers Karamazov* he had borrowed during his last visit to his family home in upstate

New York. And he had had no prior knowledge of this! His grandfather had been in his early fifties when his grandmother had given birth to Jeremy's father, and had died before Jeremy himself was born. He'd been told that his grandfather had been a humble landlord in the city. Though he had no inkling of the truth until a month or so before, he'd always felt that his mother and father had been excessively secretive—about the most insignificant things. And now with this sudden knowledge, it was as if his identity had been turned inside out. As he spoke his expression was almost bright, hopeful, his lips parted as if he was beginning to reconcile himself to what he found most confounding.

And at that moment Irina was drawn to him, not only to his story, but to the knowledge that it so bothered him. No one she knew cared about identity—duality was the reality. But to Jeremy, identity mattered. She longed to touch his hand to comfort him, but she couldn't; it wasn't in her nature, so she remained silent and listened.

"Enough talk about me. Your turn," he said suddenly, raising his wineglass to hers. His expression was so earnest, so open, Irina was moved.

"I dance," she said quietly, and told him how when she was eight, she had won five ballet lessons in a school raffle. She had been a melancholic child and didn't have many friends. Learning the basic ballet positions had made her happy. The precision of ballet had loosened something within her, causing her to realize eventually that dance was not only about movement of the body, but about movement of the mind, the heart, and yes, perhaps even the soul!

Though she has now known Jeremy for nearly a year, she is not surprised her relationship with him has remained platonic.

She's always been reserved with men. Most of her relationships have been platonic, hardly ever sexual—only on those rare occasions when she has had too much to drink. And at those times, her having imbibed too much had nothing to do with her date but with something else that was bothering her—usually it had to do with her work, not getting a role she'd longed to have. She had always felt better afterward, revived the next morning, ready to face the disappointment, as she believed her anger had been released.

She finds Jeremy's personality attractive—his warmth, his exuberance, his optimism—but physically she finds him daunting. His strong presence and his broad shoulders appear smothering; he could so easily snuff her out.

Yet Jeremy, diligent and persuasive, calls her once every month or so and asks her to go somewhere with him. And when they meet, either at his apartment, a penthouse with an expansive view of the Saint Lawrence River, or at her small flat in the older part of the city, he'll tell her he enjoys hearing her talk about her work. "Fascinating," he'll say with conviction, gazing around her living room, or if they are at his place, as he pours her a cup of espresso.

Then he'll look at her briefly, avoiding her eyes, nodding quickly, suddenly uneasy. And she'll wonder if he is in love with her, but no, this isn't possible, she'll think, for she has given him no reason to love her. She has kept her distance. Though she is compelled by his openness, his graciousness to her, she believes they are too different. She has lived her life with discipline and caution, practicing so many hours a day, purposely only becoming involved in relationships with men who will not reject her. And even though he'd been deceived about his grandfather's life, Jeremy is an optimist. Is it only through dance that she is able to reveal her exuberance for life, her passion, and her optimism? She wonders.

Interrupting her thoughts is a tinny version of "Summertime" issuing from her cell phone. Tightening the belt of her robe, she follows the music into the living room.

Pressing it to her ear, she hears Jeremy's voice, clear and buoyant. He tells her he'll be there in fifteen or twenty minutes.

Her mood sinks as she places the phone back down on the coffee table. This fluctuation in her emotions happens from time to time. Now she stands up straight, bracing herself, as if someone is drenching her with a bucket of water and she is not able to move away from the downpour.

She reaches for the package of cigarettes beneath the sofa cushion. She lights one and inhales sharply—once—twice—then immediately snuffs it out.

She has learned to adapt, to accept the mood swings and the subsequent anger. She believes she knows why this happens—her father left them when she was much too young, before she was old enough to have a sense of who he was, and her mother always has been a feeble and uninspiring person, refusing to discuss in any depth the past or Irina's father. So Irina has had to invent her father. She doesn't know his family as her mother had never gotten along with them. As a child she would sit for hours staring at the handful of photographs she had of him, moving them into different positions as if she were trying to create a mosaic. When she was in her early twenties, she chose to frame and to keep close to her the photograph now on her bedroom bureau. It most suits her invented image of him—sensitive yet defiant, wistful yet exacting.

The rumble of Jeremy's Jeep comes from the driveway below. Opening the window, she feels a rush of cold air. Her apartment is two floors up. Her voice straining, her breath visible, she calls out, "You're awfully fast."

He peers up at her, cups one gloved hand over his ear, and distorts his face to signal he cannot hear what she's saying.

After motioning for him to come up, she goes to her room and quickly dresses.

She greets him at the door with a light kiss on the lips, her bare toes nestling into the soft scatter rug and within she feels a sense of warmth—an erotic sense—something she hasn't experienced in a long while. She smiles, savoring this for a moment.

Soon, putting on her boots, she notices him staring at her, his eyes a bright blue. "I always forget how small, how petite you are," he says lightly. Then she sees his gaze shift to the slightly cracked ceiling. "There is something at the photo gallery—a surprise."

Half listening to what he's saying, she briefly imagines Jeremy as a lover. But she erases the idea from her mind as she extends her arms into the sleeves of the red woolen coat he holds open for her.

The moment they step inside the gallery, Irina understands Jeremy's surprise. There is a poster announcing the recent acquisition of a picture of the Venezuelan ballet dancer, Ramos. She once told Jeremy about him, how when she was fresh out of the dance conservatory, she had seen Ramos at a ballet in New York, a contemporary production of *Romeo and Juliet*. She had refrained from approaching him at the reception in his honor. In those days she'd been such a novice; she preferred looking at him from a distance, studying his taut, muscular body, his dark, gray-streaked hair, his fine eyes. He was the epitome of how a ballet dancer should appear, she had thought—unpretentious, sensitive, and wonderfully strong. And then there were Ramos's interpretations—imaginative, bold, and invigorating. The moment she saw him she knew he would be her muse.

With much anticipation Irina studies the full-size photograph of Ramos standing in a dance studio, wearing a tight black T-shirt, holding a jacket over one shoulder. But Ramos appears much older than when she had seen him in New York. He seems different, sterner; his hair is white, like a full, puffy cloud. He seems to be looking straight past her. She feels stunned, excluded, rejected.

"Are you surprised?" Jeremy softly asks.

"Terribly so!"

"You don't like the picture?"

"I love it!" she says, hearing her voice tremble.

She feels Jeremy's hand, tentative, warm on her shoulder and as she turns to look at him, a draft from a floor vent toys with the collar of his red flannel shirt. She looks down at his hands, the width of his knuckles. Too wide, she thinks, not in proportion to the rest of his hand.

As if he knows what she's thinking and finds humor in it, Jeremy smiles broadly.

Is it the same smile she sees when she looks at the photograph of her father propped up on her bureau? She holds Jeremy's gaze, longing for him to smile again to relive that moment of recognition. When he does, she sees it is Jeremy's smile, not the smile in the photograph. And she is pleased.

LADY OF THE WARE

As a child I went with my parents to art museums, concerts, and poetry readings. I recall the dress I wore the night I heard Beethoven's Ninth Symphony at the conservatory recital. It was light brown with a wide gold sash around the waist. The music shot through me, and during intermission I slowly sipped lemonade as if to catch my breath. And then there was that night when I was eleven and I sat with my parents at a poetry reading in the musky, dark basement of a church in Boston. It would be the last time the three of us were together. For the next day my father deserted us, ran off to California with a woman he'd met at another poetry reading, one that neither my mother nor I had attended.

That night in the church basement, the poet was a tall woman with long blond hair and deep-set brown eyes, warm and earnest, her book resting on the pulpit before her. She took a deep breath and began to read, her shoulders erect. And I felt as if she were talking to me, that she and I were the only ones in the room. The poem was called "Lady of the Night." I was inspired by her presence, the flow of her words, her fine shining eyes. This is the image I retained of her and what I clung to when my father left us the next day.

Now as I lay in bed, I looked out the hotel room window and then at the wrinkled sheet next to me with the barely visible imprint of the man I'd slept with the night before, realizing I'd never be that young again. And then I thought of how I hadn't been to an art museum, a symphony, or a poetry reading in years. I glanced about the room; it was nicer than most hotels I'd been taken to—the rug was plush, a royal blue color, the curtains were white satin, and there were gold fixtures in the bathroom.

I got out of bed and dressed, suddenly more weary than I'd been a few minutes before. It was already 10 a.m., and I needed to pick up my son from the home of a friend of mine he was staying with. She'd been unhappy about my going out with another man for the night. All she did was shake her head, her eyes teary, as I transferred my toddler from my arms to hers. And then I felt empty because I was no longer holding him.

I now sat on the edge of the bed, lowered my head, and began to cry. Soon I was sobbing, gasping, shrieking.

I heard a sharp knock at the door and then a woman's voice asked, "Are you okay in there?" I got up and opened the door.

Before me stood a tall woman, about five inches taller than I was, with long black hair that fell well past her shoulders. She was dressed in black Capri pants and a shiny silver blouse with a matching belt around her waist, her hands clasped behind her back. When I looked into her eyes, I saw compassion and determination, and I thought of the tall poetess and how tired I'd been that night at the reading, how I'd wanted to go home until I looked into her eyes as she began to read "Lady of the Night."

"I'm fine," I said, my voice sounding dull.

"You don't look fine," she said, her tone insistent. "Do you need help?"

And I began to sob some more. My head down, my eyes tightly shut, I felt her put her arm around me, walk me across the rug. And then she helped me onto the white love seat, stretching out my legs. Soon I heard her running water in the bathroom. A few minutes later she put a glass in my hand. "Drink some water," she said. And after I had taken a few sips, I opened my eyes, my gaze avoiding hers. "What is your name?" she asked.

"Eveline," I said, my lips stiff from the tears that had dried at the corners of my mouth.

"Eveline," she repeated, sitting on the chair across from me, crossing her long legs, her clasped hands on her lap. "I am Tessa. Tell me what happened."

I told her I was divorced. "He abandoned me and our child," I said and began to shake. "I have no money, no job. It is a terrible life!" I cried out.

In a soft and serious voice, she said, "Like you, most of the women on my team have been challenged in one way or another."

"The women on your team?" I asked, suddenly wondering who this woman was, this stranger.

"Yes," she said. "I call them ladies of the ware."

"Ladies of the ware? What do you mean? Who are you?" I asked, hearing panic in my voice.

"We work together, sell Tupperware. Each of us has a story—that is what binds us together. Some of our stories are not complicated, not difficult, show contentment, women who want or need to earn money to support their families, successful women, successful people. Others have been through so much—illness, abuse, self-abuse. But we persevere."

"I don't understand what you are saying."

Majestically she stood up, the sun now streaming into the room. She opened her hands, small for her height, and then I saw the scar, prominent and red, on the inside of her left wrist. And I was pained. With great dignity she spoke. "I do not know if you want my help. The women on my team are in the restaurant downstairs. Would you like to join us for breakfast?" Her eyes were firm and steady. As she turned away and began walking toward the door, it struck me that she was not a lady of the night, but of the day, a morning with a harsh, bright sun. Awkwardly, I rose to follow her.

PRELUDE

had been living close to Harvard Square for five years. On that rainy Saturday afternoon, late May, I stood at a window in my apartment, watching cars splashing through the water-soaked city street, a middle-aged couple hurrying into a Chinese restaurant with a red-and-gold-painted facade, and a sidewalk musician dressed in a hooded rain slicker sitting under the awning, strumming a guitar. Soon I was restless, and decided to walk to the café at the end of the street.

During the week, I taught second grade at a nearby public school. I wasn't a very good teacher as I felt annoyed with a child if he was having trouble reading, or if he wasn't behaving. And at those times, I'd long to walk out of the classroom, leave it behind me.

When I walked into the café that afternoon, this was weighing on my mind, along with a growing awareness that I had been unable to sustain a mature relationship, that I'd never really connected with anyone.

With my head down, covered by the hood of my jacket, I opened the heavy glass door of the café. Once inside I saw there were only two other customers. Then I heard a vaguely familiar voice ordering a cappuccino. Going over to the counter, I stood next to a man with pensive blue eyes and a wet trench coat and was startled to realize that I was almost, but not fully, certain of his identity. I continued to stare at him to be sure he was who I thought he was. I tried to put the pieces together, to match the voice with the presence, with the personality. He noticed me gazing at him and I smiled nervously.

When he saw me he was taken aback, his hand swaying as if he was about to lose his balance, though he regained his composure in a matter of seconds.

For the longest time he looked at me, his gaze hesitant, though curious. His mouth was slightly open. I didn't recall his reticence; it was something he'd learned over the past years, or maybe it had always been part of him. I simply had not known him well enough to comprehend who he really was. His eyes fastened on mine, and with a heavy voice he acknowledged it. "We know one another."

"Yes, you are Robert," I said slowly, blushing from the memory of my youth and inexperience when I went to bed with him all those years ago, though we were half-drunk.

"And you are Jocelyn," he said, carefully. "It was about ten years ago."

My heart began to race as I felt the past overtaking the present.

We moved toward a small table in the far corner. Outwardly we were hesitant, mannerly, yet on a deeper level we were quite certain of each other.

The café, usually sunny and crowded, was nearly empty, damp and dark today. Our table was covered with an unopened newspaper. Robert placed it on a chair, then turned toward me, his expression intent. He'd become more distinguished over the past ten years. No longer was he a precocious and impetuous twenty-one-year-old. In his early thirties now, he carried himself like a man nearing forty. It was his overall reserve I found enticing, as I'd experienced years of exposing myself to a few lovers, revealing to them the very depths of who I believed I was. From the start Robert's caution relaxed me, as I knew I never would have to disclose to him any more of myself than was necessary.

We walked toward the high-rise building next to the café where he'd recently purchased a condominium. Standing apart, riding the elevator, we were familiar and at the same time disassociated from each other. Robert looked up at the lighted ceiling and, staring at him, I recalled in flashes our last meeting, his broad naked shoulders, and his earnest expression.

He shook off the water from his umbrella before putting his key into the lock. The apartment was cluttered from his recent move, though the piles of books and boxes were neat and orderly—it was as if I'd come home.

"It is coincidental, our meeting again after all this time," he said, repeating what he had said to me in the café, but sounding more doubtful. He caught my gaze.

"You don't believe in coincidence, fate?" I asked, my voice sounding high-pitched. I remembered the stories about his mother and her Spanish lover, wondering, or perhaps even assuming, that because of her he'd become distrustful of women.

"Yes and no," he said, frowning. He took my jacket and gently placed it over the back of a small wooden chair in the living room.

"I do," I said, fervently. "I believe in destiny, or maybe I should say self-destiny."

He poured a glass of wine for me, and then took a bottle of beer for himself from the refrigerator. As we sat next to each other on the sofa in the middle of the room—he had not yet arranged his furniture properly—we talked about what we each were doing. He said he was a history professor, waiting to be tenured. And I told him about my work, how dissatisfied I was with it.

We were silent for a while. I got up and went over to the window, saw that it was no longer raining.

He came and stood behind me. Softly, he asked, "Are you with someone now?"

"No," I said, turning around. "Are you?"

He shook his head, his eyes avoiding mine.

"Will you stay?" he asked with much hesitation in his voice.

"Of course," I said. As he kissed me, I smelled the musky scents of beer and espresso on his breath; I pressed my hand against his neck to hold him close, felt the dampness in his hair.

We married two years later, almost to the date. Lust is a funny thing—antithetical to passion—its silence is what reverberates most, like the stillness in the air before a storm.

HALLOWEEN

Rain struck the windowpanes, forming rivulets, blurring my view of the bare oak and stone cottage across the road, the For Rent sign tilting over—it was as if I were trapped in a dream.

Restless, as the school day had ended, I sat at the desk in my second-grade classroom, a lesson plan book before me, realizing there was only winter to look forward to. Two months earlier, Robert and I had decided we would no longer try to have a child. After seven years, I was pleased with this choice, naïvely so. For instead of becoming more flexible and resolute, our life together was losing its elasticity. I'd always thought we were for the most part an open-minded couple—was that not our strength? We genuinely believed we were understanding and broad-minded toward each other and the world. But we had begun to change; we were becoming less accepting, more judgmental of friends and acquaintances.

Now when Robert paced in his study, his usual warm gaze was strained and uncertain. He was dissatisfied with anything he wrote. And I was becoming more and more impatient with him, with everyone. Our life had come to a standstill, though neither of us would admit that it had. Instead, we remained insistent that we were going forward with our pursuits, that we were living an exciting and challenging life as a couple and as individuals. The more we deluded ourselves, the more restrained we were toward each other.

On that rainy November afternoon, I looked down at the lesson plan book and began to write. I preferred a book to a computer; it was something tangible, not virtual, something I could touch, bend, and fold over. I liked the feel of a pencil in my hand as I wrote down the lessons for the coming week, printing neither assiduously nor too carelessly, but calmly, perhaps a little distractedly.

Except for the sound of the rain, there was near silence in the room. The building was brick and old, always overheated, and from time to time I'd hear a relentless pounding coming from the radiator.

One student remained in the classroom. He was so quiet I'd nearly forgotten he had not yet gone home. His name was Billy. He was a shy, sullen child, and surprisingly small for his age, as his parents were tall. They were intellectuals of sorts, I think, or they presented themselves as such. I didn't really know them. Often during class Billy would rest his head on the desk as if he felt too tired to do more work. I'd leave him alone—I believed there was nothing false or precocious about him. Yet despite his lack of guile, he was the only child that year I did not feel at ease with. There was always one in every class. Quick at learning to read words, difficult ones, he wasn't interested in the content of a story or the characters. I wondered if his parents had not spent much time reading to him.

Students like Billy stymied me; as direct as he appeared, I knew he was not what he seemed. There was much brewing beneath the surface. And as I was only a middling teacher, I was not insightful enough to help him. A more skilled teacher would have helped him focus more on his work than on his sadness. I was too respectful of his mood, never wanting to intrude on it.

At the class Halloween party the previous week, Billy had been the only student who had refused to wear a costume. And because of this, my eyes had been on him constantly that day. I had been afraid his classmates would treat him as an outcast. He had sat quietly at his desk, three cupcakes neatly placed before him, while the other children roamed about, their faces flushed, their voices high-pitched, excited, wrapped pieces of candy spilling off the tops of their desks.

While Billy now waited for one of his parents, he played with the Legos I'd given him. The ticking of the old clock on the wall made me more aware of the passing time. I was concerned I might be late meeting a friend.

Soon I noticed he was crying. He sat on the floor with his hands folded, the box of Legos next to him, tiny pieces scattered across the linoleum.

Just then I heard a sound at the door. I turned around and saw Billy's father standing on the threshold, holding a closed umbrella. He was tall and thin with dark, ponderous eyes and a bemused expression; his complexion was pale as if he were recovering from a bad flu. He appeared to be in his late thirties; his expression exuded confidence, yet the way he only smiled halfway, I wondered if there was a trace of cynicism about him. There was some character to his face, not the kind that reveals an ethical nature, but rather the type that suggests experience, hard won. Before that day I'd only seen him from a distance, waiting next to his car for Billy at the end of the school day while I stood at the front door of the school. Billy's mother was the one who had come to the parent-teacher conference. Looking me straight in the eye, she had asked me direct questions about her son. Whenever I attempted to make an excuse for his lack of progress in certain areas, she interrupted and instead gave her opinion.

From the school records, I knew Billy's father was a freelance journalist, that he was the one who had been named to pick Billy up from school every day. I believed his first name was Max. Billy's mother was a research scientist who worked in a lab at a Boston hospital.

Now Max was an intrusion in my secure and well-organized classroom, his presence like an unexpected chilly breeze on an otherwise balmy day.

"Come now, Billy," he called, avoiding my studied gaze. His voice was abrupt. Billy ran to him, and soon I heard them walking down the hallway, pausing after each step.

I next saw Max the day before the December break. He presented me with a bouquet of yellow roses, a dozen of them wrapped in cellophane. This was not unusual, as many parents would send gifts for me before the holidays began. But usually it was a child who would hand me a box of candy, homemade cookies, or flowers.

Beneath his open beige trench coat he wore a dark blue suit. There was a dull clink, his gold watch hitting mine as he handed me the flowers. He looked away, and as he did I studied him; he had a longish nose, and there was an impatience about him, a restlessness.

As the children, carrying presents and laughing, began to leave the room, he told Billy to wait for him at the front door.

Soon I heard another group of children walking down the corridor past my classroom, chanting, "It's snowing, it's snowing." I looked across the room and out the window at snowflakes falling in large white clumps onto the roof of the stone cottage house. When I turned to thank him, he was gone. But the flowers were still on my desk where I'd placed them. I picked them up and pressed them to my chest, the cellophane wrapper crackling.

Two weeks later, on a cold late December day, the window-panes were laced with ice as I paced in my bedroom, feeling confined by the weather. When the phone rang, I called out to Robert that I'd take the call.

I was not surprised to hear Max's voice. I had expected that he would call. I spoke quietly, concerned that my words would disturb Robert, who was in the next room, writing an abstract. I thought he might detect something in my tone, hesitation in my voice, for usually when I spoke with a parent of one of my students, I was confident, sometimes edgy.

Max apologized for the time he was late picking up Billy from school. Over the phone he sounded almost businesslike. He talked for a while, and I don't remember what he said, just that his drawling voice expressed words that did not seem to connect. But in retrospect, it was my own thought process that was erratic; I was too anxious to listen. Then he asked if he could meet with me. I said I could set up a parent-teacher conference. And he said no, not for that reason.

"Why?" I asked. "What is the purpose? I am your child's teacher."

"Because you are my child's teacher, because I am lonely, because my wife and I live separate lives."

"Why?" I asked again, as if I had not heard his words, listening only to the insistence and longing in my own voice. For Max, in his subtle way, had conveyed to me that there was nothing to be uplifted about in life. There was only the present, no past, no future, and no false hope. I was drawn to him because of the black-and-white quality of his beliefs—there was no mystery, no confusion. You weren't encouraged, but neither would you be disappointed.

Later, I agreed to meet him. It was a Saturday in late February. Robert had gone to a conference in Vermont for the weekend. Before he left that morning, he looked at me in a quizzical way and asked if everything was okay. I nodded energetically. I was disappointed he didn't see through me; Robert was usually perceptive in a practical, encompassing sort of way.

That afternoon I took the subway into the city and met Max at a Chinese restaurant. After lunch we got into his car and he drove back to our town, to the stone cottage across from the school. The For Rent sign had been removed.

Inside there were three rooms. A small kitchen with a narrow stove and a microwave above it; a sitting room with an oval-shaped braided rug and a rocking chair, the front legs scuffed, so still as if no one had sat in it in years; and a bedroom.

The bedroom was suffused with a mellow golden light from the mid-afternoon sun; the spread on the bed was a soft cotton quilt, a pumpkin color. And I thought of Halloween, how much I disliked the holiday when I was a child because those you knew hid behind masks and you were never certain of someone's identity—even your own when you looked at yourself in a mirror wearing a disguise.

When I dropped my pocketbook on the floor, the sound echoed, and I felt the cold and unwelcoming strap against my leg.

Max went over to the window, closed the blinds. The light in the room was dimmer now, casting shadows over the pillows, the table beside the bed. So familiar, as if I'd been there before.

As he came toward me, I saw uncertainty in his expression, a shadow crossing his face, darkening the skin beneath

his eyes. When he met my gaze, I was less doubtful, drawn to
his uncertainty.

I turned to him, detached yet intensely willing, and patted
down the collar of his trench coat.

My heart raced, my throat felt dry, my face felt frozen. I'd
never been more afraid of his dark sensuality and yet so intrigued by it at the same time.

"You are a hedonist!" I cried out, tears springing to my
eyes.

Max removed his coat and tossed it over a chair. He undid
his watch and dropped it onto the table, the same watch that
had clinked against mine when he handed me the roses that
day in the classroom.

His back to me, he hunched his shoulders forward, slowly undressing. I watched in a concentrated, curious way, just
standing there, my foot touching the pocketbook. My coat was
open and I did not move, curious about his desire, his nature.

As he came toward me, his body long, loose, jarring,
I studied him as if I was holding a piece of charcoal for the
first time, uncertain how to draw his form. When he pressed
against me, I awkwardly stroked his taut shoulder. He took
my hand, and together we went over to the bed. I sat on the
edge of the mattress; he knelt before me and with steady hands
unbuttoned my blouse. Then he raised his lips to my mouth,
his tongue against mine. I closed my eyes, my hands shaking
against his chest, hoping to push him away.

When I got home, I showered, letting the water run over me
for the longest time, and put my face directly under the show-
erhead so that the flowing stream hit my eyelids. I knew I must
flee because I no longer trusted myself, the person I met again
today, whom I'd not seen in a long time.

I took the next week off from school, telling Robert and the principal that I had hurt my back while moving a file cabinet. I needed to rest. While Robert was at work, I browsed through his professional journals. He had sabbatical time coming to him.

At the end of the week, sometime during the afternoon, I found what I'd been looking for. There was an advertisement in one of the journals for a historian specializing in American colonial history to teach a class for two semesters at a college on the Gulf Coast of Florida. Yes, I thought, Robert would be able to finish his book.

When I showed it to him, he was sitting at his desk in his cramped, tidy office on the second floor of our home. He looked it over carefully and said, "It seems as if it might suit us. I need to work on my book and you need a break, don't you?" Yet I could not read his expression.

He put down the journal on his desk and looked out the window. "Are you back, Jocelyn?" he asked in a quiet voice.

"Yes," I said, ardently. And threw my arms around his neck. He remained still.

I refused to see Max again. A babysitter now picked Billy up from school. She seemed like a thoughtful, sensitive young woman, and I wondered if Max had propositioned her as well. He wouldn't have had any qualms about doing so.

After dismissing my class, I stood in front of the school, the early March wind whipping my coat, and watched the babysitter take Billy's hand. And then I looked across the road at the stone cottage house, the For Rent sign still missing, and thought of my classroom, how it was on the day of the yearly Halloween party, all the sweat and confusion.

DESIRES

Frank Marinelli, blinded by the sudden, intense sunlight streaming past the trees, puts on his dark glasses. It is a quiet Saturday afternoon, late June. Breaking the silence is the distant sound of a dog's heavy panting coming from outside the small, leafy park. Wistful and uneasy from the heat and their recent quarrel, he turns away from the light and toward his wife, Amanda, who is sitting under a willow some yards away with an open book in her lap. There's a pensive expression on her long, narrow face, a trace of movement, an unsettledness in her slightly raised shoulders.

Last night when Frank returned home from work, Amanda was waiting for him at the door, her arms crossed and her expression wary, as if he were hours late and had not called to explain. As he bent to kiss her, she lowered her head to avoid him, tucked one hand inside the pocket of her blue jeans and pulled out a crumpled yellow check. It was the check his parents had sent a month before for his and Amanda's fifth wedding anniversary.

"I found this behind the desk," Amanda said, her chin

raised but her eyes downcast. Frank felt guilty, then anxious. "Why didn't you tell me?" she asked, her voice straining.

He walked past her into the kitchen, opened the refrigerator door and reached for a bottle of beer. Without looking at her, he answered, "I didn't know what you'd think. They want us to buy a house . . . to help out . . . They don't want us to feel left out . . . they want grandchildren . . . I don't know."

He turned around and looked directly at Amanda—her anguished expression, her fine, wheat-colored hair brushing her shoulders, her penetrating stare, the tiny zigzag scar between her brows—a reminder of a childhood mishap.

"Amanda, it seems as if everyone is earning lots of money, except us."

When he looked up, Amanda's eyes were closed, as if she were in pain. And he thought of the first time he saw her, how her lids had been lowered in the same way as she had scooped ice cream out of a large aluminum tin. He had been sitting at a table in the ice cream shop with his friends, watching her closely, wishing she was waiting on their table.

Bringing him back to the present was her voice, slicing him, like a pair of scissors tearing open a sheet. "We can't accept this check, Frank. You've been…you expect too much. We'll buy a house . . . eventually. You'll get a promotion at the firm. It takes time. I realize there are many other lawyers, but you'll do something to make yourself noticed. And I have only one semester left of school. We can wait." She opened her steady, brown eyes and he turned away.

Queasy, disoriented, he didn't agree with her; this money was owed to him. He'd been a diligent, respectful son; he had taken time off from law school for a few years when his father needed help with his business. He felt he was still paying a price for this; he would be further ahead in his career if he had not done so. Younger women and men were receiving promotions because they had been at the firm longer than Frank. And in the past, Amanda had accepted money gratefully, easily from his parents. But this time it was much more than they'd ever before offered. Frank took a deep breath.

"You see, Frank, you feel things are owed to you, and I don't."

Later, still in the kitchen, weary from arguing, Amanda said in a quiet, thoughtful voice, "Our temperaments are different. You are more accepting than I am, Frank. It isn't in my nature to easily trust, to believe people are altruistic at heart." She creased her forehead in a way that caused her to appear older than thirty.

And the same old fear surfaced: a belief that Amanda would suddenly and unexpectedly leave him because of what she called the difference in their temperaments.

After dinner, she went into the bedroom and Frank sat alone at the kitchen table. He loosened his tie and thought about nothing, just felt guilty for not having shown her the check. It had been written out in both their names.

After a while, he ambled into their bedroom. Amanda was not sleeping, as he expected, but lying in bed reading, only a sheet wrapped round her body, her knees raised, the light from the reading lamp illuminating a page of her book.

Frank lay down next to her, his head grazing her arm; she nodded without looking at him. He turned his body toward Amanda. Sighing, she closed the book. Extending her arms around his shoulders she embraced him so tightly he could feel the thumping of her heart. Then she fell back onto the pillow.

They made love shyly, a bit awkwardly, and Frank was saddened by the experience. He knew they'd been intimate to try and quell the tension between them, but it remained, like the steady hum of an unseen insect.

Amanda slept and Frank followed the occasional shadow

crossing the ceiling from a passing car. He had felt the same way the first time they had made love. Even then he was sad because he had believed he'd not been able to penetrate her quietude.

Alone in the park with Amanda, his hands inside the pockets of his blue jeans, Frank now quietly strolls toward her. He longs to enjoy the beauty of this early summer morning, the fine smell of grass and flowers, but he can't at a moment like this. It is impossible for him to relax when there's conflict between them.

When he reaches her, she looks up. "What is it, Frank?" she asks, cupping a hand over her close, spidery brows. A soft breeze rustles the leaves above her head.

The expression on her face, her lips in a half smile, her questioning tone reminds him of that night a few months before their wedding. As they sat in his parked car, close to the beach, he grasped her hand and looked out at the ocean, the gray-black sky reflected in the coal-colored waters, the clouds high and wispy. No other cars were parked near them. When Amanda turned to him, the glare from the flashlight of a passing beachcomber illuminated her face just as she said, "I've decided to take your name, Frank." But she spoke as if asking a question.

And he answered spontaneously, "But your name, Hopkins, is shorter, simpler, easier.

She nodded, then responded in a clear voice, no trace of a question in her words. "Marinelli sounds happier," she said in a firm tone.

But after five years, is she happier? he wonders. Is he? How can they be when they want different things? But do they? She knows what she wants, but he isn't certain about his desires, how he wants his life to unfold, he thinks.

He now sits next to her, and she puts the book down on the grass. He takes off his sunglasses and impulsively kisses her open dry lips, surprising her. "Oh, Frank," she says, a trace of passion in her voice, and gently pushes him away. He thinks she wants to say something to him and he feels uneasy.

She looks away from him and picks up her book. It is a hardcover copy of Faulkner's *Light in August*, the same book she was reading in bed last night. After reading a bit, she looks up at him. "Frank, what should we do?" she asks in her steady, clear way. Her lashes lower—pale.

He is stunned by her question. Will she leave him now? he wonders, and his heart begins to race.

"About the check, Frank? What will we do?"

He feels momentarily relieved, but he is much less convinced about what to do about the check than when they were arguing last night. "I don't know, Amanda."

The park gate clicks open. A large greyhound trots in. Frank smiles, forgetting for a moment his fears about his marriage, admiring the dog's grace and speed.

He glances at Amanda, who isn't partial to animals. He picks up her hand and squeezes it. They get up as the dog approaches, growling at them.

Frank bemusedly watches, wondering what the hound will do next.

The animal nips the back of Amanda's white, sleeveless shirt; Frank feels her warm hand slip from his grasp, hears the book plop onto the ground.

Wanting to help, but suddenly overcome with anger and resentment at her fixed sense of right and wrong, her strong will, he stares, paralyzed, as the dog chases Amanda round the willow.

Amanda stumbles over a large jagged rock and falls backward onto the bright green ground. As the dog hovers over her, she closes her body into a fetal position.

His passion for her overpowering him, Frank lunges over and grabs the dog by the collar, feels the animal's coarse fur bucking his grip. He believes he will forever be able to hold back this growling, flailing creature; his heart pounding as he fully imagines what could have happened to Amanda.

He turns his head and sees Amanda crawling toward the tree. She leans against the trunk, her arms clutching her raised knees.

Is she crying? Frank wonders. There may be one or two tears covering her already shiny eyes, but he cannot tell. Amanda rarely cries.

"Frank," she calls out in a high, nervous voice and points towards the gate.

Before looking over, Frank takes a firmer grip on the dog's collar. He sees a man walking towards them, the owner perhaps—a short, bulky man wearing dark glasses, who suddenly snaps his fingers.

The dog tears loose from Frank's grip, leaping toward the man.

As the man and dog leave the park, Frank goes to Amanda, sits next to her, and takes her hand. He realizes how much he does and doesn't love her—how much he fears who he is, what he is becoming.

Amanda looks up, stares at him as if he is someone she does not recognize, but soon this expression passes.

"Thanks, Frank," she says, her voice shaky, her eyes filled with gratitude.

Frank doesn't know what to do, what to say; he just squeezes her hand some more. Both of them are silent, awed by the experience.

After what seems like the longest time, he feels her hand stroking the side of his face. She whispers in his ear, "We will accept your parents' check; we will buy a house."

As if Amanda's will can make something right, acceptable, Frank thinks. He shrugs, mouths the words, "We'll see." And he thinks of the day they were married, dancing with her before they bid good-bye to their parents. Wedding guests had formed a circle around them. "Blue Moon" was the song. Amanda was wearing a teal dress, a cotton shift that fell straight to her knees. When he held her close, she briefly relaxed in his arms but soon pulled away. It was because they were surrounded by friends and family, and not alone, he'd assumed.

He now looks over at her, her puzzled expression. As he stands, he takes her hand, intending to pull her to her feet. At first, he feels resistance, but soon he sees how Amanda allows him to help her up in that familiar, hesitant way they have of yielding to one another.

Salzburg and Vienna

I

Orange streaks of light pale; the sky slowly darkens. It is late October, early evening. The air is brisk—I walk quickly toward the subway.

Near Lincoln Center, I pass a group of tourists standing in line close to a cavernous bus, silver with Kansas plates. A sudden strong wind blows; a palm-sized digital camera hits the sidewalk. I step away.

As I make my way down the subway stairs, I hear the sound of an approaching train. I step into the car and the doors close behind me. Once I find a seat, I pull a past issue of *Smithsonian* from my briefcase and begin to read an article on Pompeii. The golden-hued photographs, vivid and enticing, divert my attention from the text.

Soon I realize I have lost track of time. I look up. Sitting next to me is a jovial-looking man wearing a loose beige raincoat. He has a round face, a fair complexion, a smooth high forehead and small gray eyes, twinkling at one moment, appearing vague and unyielding at the next. There is something both exuberant and repressed about him, as with those who long to experience life fully, passionately, yet at the same time are fearful of doing so. He catches my gaze, asks if I know what time it is. His voice is high-pitched, excitable, yet his diction is clear and precise.

I show him the hour on my cell phone, and ask him if he is from New York. The train jolts to a stop.

A pleased expression crosses his face. He promptly tells me he is from Austria—Vienna.

"I visited Vienna ten years ago; Salzburg too," I say.

"Mozart and Salzburg, Freud and Vienna," he says energetically, as if responding to an oral quiz. I sense he is mocking me.

Turning, he gazes into the dark tunnel. In a quiet and confidential voice he says there is an old Austrian saying—the narrower the valley, the more narrow-minded the people. Now when he looks at me, his eyes are soft and wistful.

I am not certain he is Austrian, or what he has told me is an old Austrian saying. Despite his cheery presence, I find him haunting. I repeat it to myself over and over: "The narrower the valley, the more narrow-minded the people," trying to find a clear major note or theme in his message, but I am at a loss. His words disorient me. All I realize is his saying may not be as simple as it seems. Yet his presence loosens my memory, and I recall my own trip to Austria.

II

It was mostly dark and silent inside the jetliner bound for Salzburg. All the overhead lights were out, except for the small bulb above my seat. Next to me, Julian slept, earphones around his neck. He breathed slowly, thoroughly, rhythmically, like a polonaise; his long lean body curled up, his drooping head resting on my arm. His presence was soothing. I studied his lips full and even, his brows, high and wispy. Lightly I tapped the tip of his long narrow nose.

I thought about the day I first met him. It was the previous September, a coffee shop near Carnegie Hall. I sat alone at the bar, attempting to read a biography of Liszt. At first I was diverted by the sound of rain striking the large window before me. But soon I became so absorbed in what I was reading I did not realize someone had come to sit next to me. When I felt a firm tap on my shoulder, I turned and met his kind, inquisitive expression. His dark hair was wet and sleek, and he carried the scent of rain as if he'd just splashed himself with aftershave. And within I experienced the same warm sensation I felt whenever I was told a complex and poignant secret.

Pointing to my book, he asked if I had a particular interest in Liszt and told me that though he didn't play an instrument, he always had had a predilection for the classical; he liked to listen to it more than to any other type of music. As he spoke, I looked down at the book, at the cover photograph of a painting of Liszt, noticed how it resembled him: It was in the eyes, the blue-green color and the almond shape. I commented on the likeness, and he studied it for a while before agreeing.

Now, nine months later, we were flying to Salzburg because Julian, a journalist, had been assigned to write an article about Austrian life, past and present. He intended to interview a man named Herbert Glaus, owner of the Glaus Mountain Resort, thirty miles outside of Salzburg, where we would be staying courtesy of Herbert. Herbert had lived in the Alps most of his life, and had a doctorate in Austrian history. He was now semi-retired from teaching.

Herbert had contacted colleagues of his in Salzburg so that Julian would be able to meet with them. At the end of our trip we would drive to Vienna. Lately Julian had been reading some of Freud's writings, and was still debating whether or not to include the psychoanalyst in his article. Regardless, he had decided to visit the apartment where Freud had lived, the Freud Haus.

With much trepidation, I had agreed to accompany Julian on this trip. I was drawn to him, his intricate personality. Yet at the same time he puzzled me. I thought it odd he never spoke of his parents; there was tension in our relationship because of this. All he told me was that he was an only child. He called it a curse.

Whenever I inquired about his mother or father, what he would say in a half-joking, half-serious way, his eyes darting, was that they were alive. I was compelled, bewildered, and subtly thrilled by Julian's evasiveness.

And on his part, I'm sure he could not understand why I was happy working behind the counter in a music shop after my degree in music history. He thought I should apply to graduate school. I would tell him I had plenty of time to decide about my future. What was the rush? I needed to explore life some more before I chose what to do next.

Over the intercom, the pilot announced we would be landing in Munich for about an hour, a brief stopover before continuing on to Salzburg. A minor problem with the air-conditioning, he said in an impassive voice.

Julian, half-awake now, slowly stood up and reached for his canvas bag in the overhead compartment. Unzipping the bag, he pulled out the maps I'd seen him carefully pack the night before. He chose one, sat down, and opened it up, ironing out the folds with his fist.

It was a map of the Munich area. Julian pointed to Dachau, not very far away. He gazed directly at me, his dark, heavy lashes flickering, his voice husky from sleep. He asked, "Laura, we can pick up a car in Munich? Then after poking about for a while, we'll drive into Austria. This side trip to Dachau will add dimension to my article on Austria."

Thirty minutes later, we were standing in front of a car rental booth in the Munich airport. Julian, using his basic college German, attempted to communicate with the tall woman behind the stand.

Soon we were driving towards Dachau. Julian tightly grasped the steering wheel, lowered his head, looked straight ahead, didn't say a word. He was too weary to speak, and so was I—it was insane, rushing out of Munich after an eight-hour flight with barely any sleep. But that is what I relished most about Julian—his impulsivity: highly ethical, surprisingly thoughtful, always based on a passion of one sort or another.

A misty haze permeated Dachau. The fog was so thick it was difficult to see, to get a sense of its entirety. At the visitor center we were told about two buildings, the Memorial Museum and the barracks. I felt uneasy as I was not able to clearly see what was in the distance.

I visited the Memorial Museum alone while Julian walked over to the barracks to videotape the quarters where the victims had slept.

I wandered only halfway through the museum; the blown-up black-and-white photographs of children, women, men, dressed in prison stripes or ordinary clothing, stepping toward death, frightened me. I left, unable to tolerate any more.

Outside the museum, I heard and saw Americans, about ten or so, most wearing sweatshirts on this unseasonably cold day, some, like Julian, with camcorders in hand, and others, just roaming about looking sad—no, devastated—faces lowered, hands clenched. I needed to leave the place; there was no solace. In the distance, through the fog, I saw Julian coming towards me, his form wavering, disconnected.

Within twenty-four hours we were settled in the Glaus Mountain Resort, sheltered in the Alps, thirty miles south of Salzburg. It was a drizzly, damp day and gray clouds floated low, nearly touching the ground.

Inside our studio apartment, the paneling on the walls was a dark wood. A grayish light filtered into the room through the parting in the thick, beige drapes.

The bed was in the center of the room—on it were two soft pillows and a white cotton quilt. Julian, splayed across the mattress, was paging through a travel book. He bit vigorously into an apple, his dark head pushing into the whiteness of the quilt.

I went to him and slowly began to unbutton his shirt; he continued to read, his expression focused, serious. Then suddenly he dropped his book and took my hand, fervently kissing my palm.

The next morning was warm and soothing. We swam in the glass-enclosed pool on the first level of the resort. Outside, the sky was a vibrant blue, and the Alps imposing and craggy.

Julian swam to the end of the pool, slapped his hands against the tile, lifted himself out of the water. His gold trunks clung to his hips and his back was moist; his shoulders arched backward, as if he wanted to rid himself of some heavy burden.

I followed him out of the pool, across the blue-tiled floor, through the opening in the glass doors to the outside Jacuzzi. We descended into the bubbling, steamy water, and stretched out our arms across the rim. It was quite early. No one else was

around. Sunlight stroked the tops of our heads and the surface
of the water. Julian edged close to me. Playfully he pulled at
the strap of my bathing suit; we kissed, and then laughed, as if
drunk.

Dizzy with desire, we stepped out of the Jacuzzi, retrieved
our towels by the pool, and walked to the elevator.

In our room, we undressed in silence. On the soft, white
quilt, we made love at first slowly, then ardently, as if we had
not been together in months.

After lunch, a little dazed from the wine we had drunk,
we walked through the small village. When we returned to the
resort, we bumped into Herbert Glaus in the lobby. He was sitting on the sofa next to the reception desk, reading a newspaper, nodding his head to the sound of "My Favorite Things," the
music coming from behind the front desk. Despite the warm
weather, he was wearing a short-jacketed wool suit; his face
was thin and drawn, his moustache dark and trim. When he
saw us, he stood up and smiled.

Julian and Herbert made plans to meet for another interview. After a time was mutually agreed upon, Herbert, in his
reserved way, suggested that we hike the Alps—they are seductive, simple, he enunciated in his careful English, before resum-
ing his position on the sofa.

The next day we drove into Salzburg: narrow streets,
broad squares, clanging church bells, and a medieval castle
that stood on a hill above the city. After walking about for an
hour or so, we sat on a bench in the Mozartplatz. It was close to
noon. A few feet away was a statue of the musician, and behind
us, across the street from the square, was an American Express
office. Julian spread his arms across the top of the bench, closed
his eyes, and tilted up his chin at the blazing sun. He appeared
to be resting, but I felt the usual, mild tension between us suddenly increase.

I soon heard the haunting strains of Liszt's *Faust Symphony*—an orchestra, a rehearsal perhaps—the music wafting to us from around the bend.

Julian opened his eyes, looked over at me. "Isn't that Liszt? Become an expert on Liszt," he continued insistently. "You possess a natural enthusiasm. Why don't you teach?"

"Academic study doesn't interest me. Enjoying Liszt's music does not have to be an intellectual exercise—I will not allow you to ruin my appreciation of his work," I answered firmly and glanced across the square at the long line of people waiting for the next *Sound of Music* bus tour.

"But your family—they all have professions. Why are you trying to run from what you are?" he asked, his tone insistent, demanding.

"I am different," I said, thinking of my ophthalmologist father, well respected for his research in the field; my mother, a visually discerning landscape architect; and my sister, a conscientious surgeon-in-training.

He spun away from me and threw up his arms. "You are disorganized!"

He spoke with such abandon and hostility that the pigeons loitering close to us suddenly, briskly flew away. The sun cast a halo-like light over Julian's dark head.

I stood up and asked, slowly, firmly, "What and who are you?"

He looked up at me; his expression was sad, hopeless. I walked away from him. He followed.

One week later we were speeding toward Vienna in the rented car, the Alps in the distance now. Julian wanted to reach the Freud house before it closed for the day. It was at least a three-hour drive, and it was a little after noon. The next day we would

fly home from Vienna to New York. Our plane was scheduled
to leave at eight in the morning. So we would have to see the
Freud house that afternoon.

For the past fifteen minutes, Julian had tenaciously been
pushing buttons, switching channels on the radio. He settled
at last on a station that was playing a jazz version of the "Blue
Danube Waltz."

We had not communicated much since our argument in
the Mozartplatz seven days before, and had not done much
sightseeing, though Julian had been avidly reading books
about Austria, and had driven alone into Salzburg nearly every
afternoon to interview Herbert's colleagues.

Herbert became my confidant during this short period.
We'd have lunch together while Julian was away. And so, in a
figurative sense, I did hike the Alps with Herbert. The experience was not as seductive and simple as he had implied. Herbert, despite his fine appearance and refined speech, was a demanding and impatient lover.

As I waited for Herbert in his room, the last afternoon we
were together, I noticed on the shelf above the television set a
small wooden sculpture of a bicycle. I picked it up and slowly
fingered the wheels, recalling the summer my father attempted
to teach me to ride. I had been eight years old, and unsuccessful.
That morning in the park, Father had firmly grasped the front
bar of my blue-and-white bicycle, his hands narrow and white;
he had spoken in a pointed, pressing voice, his dark moustache
quivering, blinking his eyes in the glare of the sun. "But Laura,
you are a coordinated child; this doesn't make sense." I had
started to cry. He had walked away from me and sat on a bench
about thirty feet away. All I'd heard between my sobs was the
sound of traffic in the distance. I'd not thought about that day
in a long time, but I believed it was the day I began to realize life
was more complex than straightforward.

I was so lost in thought that I did not realize Herbert had come into the room. He was standing close to me. He gently took the wooden bicycle from my hand and placed it on the shelf. He didn't say anything. His expression was kind but fixed. Yet this last time together, I was the one who was demanding and impatient. I was surprised Herbert acquiesced.

We arrived at the Freud Haus two hours before it closed. Julian, exhausted from the drive, refused to stop first at the hotel where we would be spending the night.

In Freud's apartment, Julian squinted, attempting to read the German documents hanging on the walls. Occasionally he'd use the camcorder slung around his neck to zero in on a photograph of Freud he found compelling.

I enjoyed browsing through the house. There were many figures on display that Freud had collected: small granite-like forms, with open stances, perplexed expressions. Joyful? Anguished? I could not tell. I returned to the entrance and asked the guard if there was a connection between psychoanalysis and the figures Freud had collected.

Tall, thin, curly-haired, he was at a lectern, leaning forward, immersed in a book. Looking askance at me, his lips slowly parted. He suddenly blushed, and said he didn't know; he was studying biology.

Julian and I dined at an outdoor restaurant across from a massive stone cathedral. The small plastic table was shaky, and the linen covering nearly slipped off as the waiter cleared our plates.

When he was gone, Julian reached for my hand, loosely held it, as if he was afraid something unexpected would happen. "You slept with Herbert," he said thoughtfully.

I was surprised. My heart pounded, but I did not acknowledge the truth.

"Herbert told me. I feel responsible," he said. His voice now was intensely serious, his eyes misty.

We sat in silence for a while.

"Laura, I do not want you to be anything other than what you are." He paused, and said, "I am so drawn to you." He didn't appear happy.

I studied him, his solemn expression, his downcast eyes, and after a few moments, I said, "Why." For the first time I realized the rhetorical why in its purest sense was not a question, but a statement.

Two hours into our flight home, after a light meal, I began to read the biography of Mozart I had purchased in Salzburg at the beginning of the trip. Julian lightly tapped me on the shoulder and I fleetingly recalled that rainy September afternoon at the coffee shop near Carnegie Hall. But when I now turned toward him, he appeared quite distressed. My heart began to race.

"I have been meaning to tell you," he began, his voice filled with emotion. "My parents are in jail—it has to do with their work—violations—crimes, supposedly—white collar…" His voice trailed off, his fingers raised and fluttering, as if he'd just played on the piano a short and intricate piece written in a minor key.

That was all he said. He did not attempt to reveal any other facts or details.

Our gazes met, locked. He was, I believed, reassured.

∾

III

I last heard from Julian about five years ago. He wrote to tell me he had been named chief international correspondent for his magazine and was commuting back and forth between Rome and Vienna. In his postscript, he wrote that his parents were not longer in jail; they had been released on a technicality a few years before. He didn't elaborate.

I imagine Julian is now married to a European woman—Italian or Viennese—a sophisticated and open-minded woman.

I am not certain why we eventually stopped seeing each other. I think the end of our relationship had to do with my father becoming ill. And Julian's work was occupying more and more of his time.

I did go back to graduate school, concentrated on Liszt, received my doctorate, and now I am teaching music history at a college in the city.

My father survived his illness. When I saw him last month, he said he believed my life was now whole, as he always thought it would be. That I had become truly confident, as he knew I would. His eyes were hazy, not as penetrating and direct as before, and I thought there was a touch of irony in his voice. And I recall the words of the paradoxical Austrian, who bid me a jolly good-bye as I got off the train a few hours ago. Perhaps my father, after all, is like the Viennese.

Over the past ten years, I've been involved in a few relationships—not one of them lasted. There is a colleague of mine, a year or two younger, who has asked me several times in his lighthearted, roundabout way if I'd be interested in attending a colloquium with him on Liszt's *Dante Symphony*, in Rome, during our winter break.

I was six years old when I first saw Italy. It was summer, late June. Father was attending a month-long conference in Rome. All I remember about that trip was crossing a wide street near the Colosseum after a long lunch, and Mother dropping her handbag. Inside it was her instant camera.

The color of her purse—a rich turquoise—caught my attention, and I ran back to retrieve it. When I looked up, I saw a car a short distance away speeding toward me. Before I had a chance to register what was happening, Father rushed to my side, lifted me up, and carried me over his shoulder to the closer sidewalk. My heart pounded. I had been rescued, yet in his arms, my body swaying, I was not secured.

JACKSONVILLE

He boarded the train in Richmond at seven in the evening. It was a Friday in late February, and a snowstorm that had blanketed the northeast was heading south. He had planned to fly to Jacksonville, but upon hearing the report, the possibility of inclement weather, he decided to travel by rail. He anticipated bad news in Jacksonville.

When he walked into the dining car, he noticed her sitting alone in a booth, looking out the window. As he approached the table, she turned away from the glass as if she'd been expecting him. Hesitantly she met his gaze, her blue-green eyes glistening beneath hooded lids. Around her neck she wore a red wool scarf, wide and loose. She tilted her head to the left, her expression decided. Naïve, he thought, because of how she raised her brows.

She nodded, and he slid into the seat opposite her; he clasped his hands together, drawing attention to his left hand: no ring on his finger. He wasn't and had never been married.

He eased his head forward as if he were about to fall into prayer, and asked if could stay.

She waited before saying yes, avoiding his earnest stare.

Wearing his lined raincoat, he thought he must appear bulky to her, but he wasn't inclined to remove it. He needed the protection; it was cold in the train.

There was an empty beer bottle between them; reaching for it, she tilted the bottle forward and told him in a slow, soft voice that she was on her way to Jacksonville to visit her sick mother, whom she hadn't seen in a year. He guessed she was in her early thirties, about his age.

He told her he had a business meeting the next day. His broad hands spread out on the table. Then he said he thought he would be fired, and that it wasn't the first time. In the past he'd been told both by women he'd been involved with and by employers that he had a personality problem.

She looked up at him. No longer seeming shy, she met his gaze and smiled, her top lip narrow, her teeth small.

And he felt unburdened in some way. His problems were distant and unreal.

A few moments later the conductor slammed on the brakes, the passengers lurched forward, and she was thrown into his outstretched arms.

When everything was still, his head throbbing, he eyed the other passengers, wincing; he noticed bruises, and perhaps some broken limbs. And there she was, her arms around his neck, a scrape across her forehead.

They spent the night in a motel outside of Raleigh. They shared the same room, a room with two double beds covered in green flowery spreads.

They stayed up for the remainder of the night talking, talking about what they most feared, their voices animated now in the aftershock of their experience. She feared life, she said, holding one hand to her face—she felt as if hers had not yet begun, and the years were passing.

JACKSONVILLE   109

Standing, he gripped the back of an armchair and told her he feared losing control. He was always holding back, afraid of the consequences.

At five in the morning they began to make love. The alarm clock beside the bed rang as he stroked her bare breast. That was when she told him it was her first experience. They laughed together, and then cried.

Four hours later they shared a taxi to the airport. The highway was slick from a rainy night. But the sky was now clear and still.

That afternoon he was fired in Jacksonville, but within a few weeks he landed another job, and the following year he was married. He'd had a whirlwind romance with a flight attendant he'd met during a bumpy flight to the West Coast. He'd sought her out as one who'd been able to ease his anxiety during all the turbulence. He felt better just looking at her, watching her walk up and down the passageway, patting the back of each aisle seat.

Now he's been married for ten years, a comfortable, roomy marriage, a marriage that has had a calming effect on his life, his career. Though there are times—mostly on rainy Sunday evenings—he's melancholic and restless. Whenever these moments occur, he'll pick up a book, pretend he is reading. And he'll relive in his mind the train ride to Jacksonville, and how when the conductor had slammed on the brakes, she had sprung up and into his arms, holding onto him for life.

WADE'S TECHNIQUE

I

"You were in a dark place," she paused, then said, "Gregory."

Her voice was pensive, though he heard a slight edge in it when she spoke his name. He watched Sheila lower her head with exacting grace and look away from him.

Reluctantly he waited for her to say more.

It was early August and the air-conditioning in his high-ceilinged apartment was not working because of a power failure. All the windows had been opened to the unrelenting sound of city traffic.

Her narrow form was perfectly framed by the long window. Late afternoon light poured into the room, brightening her hazy gray eyes. Again their gazes met. Though her expression was impassive, her arms were extended in disbelief. She continued: "I believe you were in a cave. The dream was in black and white, not color."

Gregory, his heart thumping, crossed his arms and

113

moved closer, assessing her as if she were a physician providing a review of his health.

Her face was damp from the heat; the more she spoke, the more her wide-set eyes appeared spread apart. He found her voice prickly; she paused, as if each word contained a meaning separate from the sentence as a whole.

He looked past her, out the open window, at the concrete apartment buildings lining the street, and then at the stalled cars below, horns blaring into the fog of heat. And he envisioned the very same street last winter—how often cars had been just as immobilized but because of the snow—and his thoughts then drifted to the unexpected February storm. He and Sheila had spent the day together, doing errands, skating, and then dining at an Italian restaurant. When they had returned to her apartment, she had snapped open the blinds, and with lights off they'd sat on the sofa, mostly in silence, sharing a bottle of tequila, watching the thick white flakes fall profusely from the black sky. "How overwhelming," she said, her words echoing into the darkness.

"I find it calming," he responded, reflexively taking another gulp of liquor.

An hour later he studied her, the lights now on and dimmed; she waltzed about the room in that graceful-sharp way of hers, clutching the tequila bottle close to her chest, casting shadows about the room. Her usual reserved expression was animated and her hair, which she mostly wore in a French braid, was loosened, a dark, curly mass falling past her shoulders.

What proceeded, or what occurred following their first attempt at lovemaking that night, he could not recall. All he knew was that it had not happened again. They kept in contact, he guessed, because they were lonely, desirous.

"You were stuck, you couldn't move, perhaps it was mud—something viscous," she now said, raising one hand and rubbing two fingers together. She looked quizzically at him, as if expecting him to know the answer, he thought.

He uncrossed his arms and turned away, wondering what she wasn't telling him about the dream—maybe she had dreamed he had drowned in quicksand. Disquieted, he ignored her words and focused on her presence. Despite her dispassion, which he, a Midwesterner, had found inherent in other New Englanders as well, he believed she was different, ultimately hopeful.

She had called him a few hours before and had said she wanted to stop by after she finished her work at the studio. He had been discomforted by her voice; she had sounded as if she intended to relay bad news to him.

"I did not know whether or not you needed help getting out of this cave. But I think that was only the center of the dream. I'm not sure, that's what is so confusing about it," she said, raising her brows. But he believed she appeared more perspicacious than confused.

"The dream was strong, visceral. I needed to see you today, to see if you were well." She paused, and for a moment, he saw angst in her expression, yet heard a subtle tone of relief in her voice, not because he was fine, he thought, but because she had felt some sort of responsibility in telling him about the dream.

Not knowing what to make of her dream—he had always felt dissatisfied discussing someone's dreams, or recalling his own—he changed the subject. He scratched his head and told her he had been thinking of going to a movie, to escape inside an air-conditioned theater.

"I'll come with you," Sheila answered solemnly. But he thought she seemed preoccupied with the dream.

As they walked toward the cinema he effortlessly took her hand, pressing her palm, flecked with dry paint, against his.

Glancing at him, Sheila began to speak about Adam Wade, a contemporary artist known for his fine surreal landscapes. She told him a show of his would be coming to Boston in a few weeks. A balmy breeze draped a strand of loose hair across her forehead. Gray clouds appeared, and the sky was darkening quickly, suddenly. He was accustomed to her choosing a topic of conversation she knew he would disagree with and then relentlessly pursuing it.

In one quick breath he said that, as he had mentioned to her before, he had seen the artist's work and had found Wade's paintings to be desolate—hopeless—maybe bland.

Sliding her hand from his grasp, Sheila said she disagreed. She believed Wade was an expansive, innovative artist.

She walked a few paces ahead, one shoulder slightly raised. He felt a raindrop on his arm, then heard thunder in the distance; within minutes there was a downpour, water streaming down the street.

Instead of continuing in the direction of the cinema, they turned and ran in the opposite direction, back toward his apartment.

In his small kitchen he stood next to the window, the sill damp from the rain, water vigorously striking the pane. He turned away and reached for a bottle of wine from the top shelf; he heard Sheila moving about the living room, the heels of her shoes clacking against the hardwood floor.

Droplets of rain from his hair sprinkled the floor as he lowered his head and poured the wine, filling two glasses to the brim.

Eyeing Sheila through the doorway, he watched her sit on the brown corduroy sofa, cross her legs, knot them tightly together, and lean forward. She caught his stare and in response she returned to their conversation about Wade.

"It's Wade's technique," she said. "It is what I most appreciate about his work. Fine strokes, faint colors, provocative, compelling—his complexity lies in his simplicity, his ability to accept his simplicity."

"Is acceptance a propensity, or an ability?" Gregory asked as he came toward her and handed her a glass of wine. She looked up at him; he saw the black flecks in her eyes contract, her lashes moist, steady, the faint lines on her forehead more evident.

"The latter," she answered decidedly. Pausing, she asked him if he'd like to go with her to the Wade exhibit. He nodded. A truce of sorts, he thought.

He sat next to her, placed the bottle of wine on the floor, then turned halfway round and reached behind the sofa for a small pile of CDs lying on the table next to the player. He carefully placed one inside the machine. Soon jazz filtered through the room.

Glancing over at Sheila, he saw she was staring straight ahead, intently sipping her wine. Then she half smiled and raised her glass for more. Was she silently debating their conversation about Wade, or their very odd relationship? he wondered, pouring more wine into her glass.

The rich and complicated sound of Miles Davis on trumpet filled the room. Water pelted the windowpane. And soon under the spell of the thick, red wine and the heavy rain, they slid into one another's arms, then legs.

The next day, he woke early. Before him, Sheila was perfunctorily dressing, zipping up her jean shorts, stretching her arms through the holes of a sleeveless cotton jersey.

Abruptly he sat up in bed, gazing at her quick, neat movements. The bright morning light grazed the top of her head; her naturally curly hair now had a static electric look.

Their gazes locked; Sheila returned to their conversation of the previous night. She spoke about Wade, going to the exhibit—which day would be best for him? Gregory heard himself respond to her in kind.

Grasping our way back to friendship, he thought, like two people slowly, awkwardly climbing onto separate rafts after having been out dunking together in murky waters.

She told him she wanted to get to the studio early, before the heat set in.

In his bathrobe, he walked her to the door, his bare feet against the rough floor. Standing on the threshold, he gently kissed her.

He went to the window and watched her amble down the street, like a dancer in toe shoes, stepping forward on the heels of her feet. He had seen that walk before.

II

Fifteen summers earlier, twenty-year-old Gregory, following a semester of studying Dutch history in Amsterdam, had traveled on his own throughout much of Europe.

After spending the last few weeks of May in France, he had boarded a train to Berlin and then made his way west. Four days later, he arrived in a north German town. After two days there, in the June twilight, he walked slowly toward the train station. A few feet ahead he noticed a woman with a backpack and camera bag, walking on her heels, like a ballerina. But he soon lost sight of her.

After purchasing his ticket, he sat on the concrete platform, his backpack at his side, and waited for the train. Across the tracks he saw a band of four accordion players who had emerged, it seemed, from nowhere. Without introduction they began to play hollow, discordant-sounding music.

For a moment Gregory felt lost. To orient himself, he turned away, and saw that next to him was the woman who had been walking ahead of him moments before.

When she noticed him looking at her, she stared directly at him, not flinching. Her eyes were a deep brown without any specks of light, her chin narrow and firm. She asked if he was an American.

"Yes," he said. She shifted her body so that she was now facing him, then tilted her head to the side, her eyes attentive.

She told him she was from this town, from north Germany, and, pointing to her camera bag, she added that she studied photography. Was he traveling south? Before he had a chance to answer, she told him her name was Karin. She leaned forward and said in her fine English, "It is spelled with an *i*."

Their first night together they spent in a Munich inn run by a tall woman in her late fifties, strongly built. As they checked in Gregory noticed the proprietress wore a Playboy bunny–shaped key dangling from a long silver chain round her neck, resting atop her full chest. Her English was good, but heavily accented. When she placed the key to the room in Gregory's palm, her hand felt coarse, and he took note of her haughty expression. After taking a few steps, Karin at his side, he looked back and saw that the proprietress now appeared wistful. He was disoriented—was her necklace an omen of some sort?

Over the next few days, whenever he saw the proprietress checking someone in at the front desk or clearing coffee cups in the hotel lobby, the bunny key dangling from the chain, he forced himself to ignore her strong back, her tight, firm movements.

Gregory never parted from Karin during the two and a half weeks they spent together. Her stark honesty was what he liked best about her. And there was her dark, shiny hair, her long bangs looping over her brows, her naturally sallow coloring, her intense expression made more so by her high cheekbones and narrow chin.

They would sit naked together on the hard, small bed. He would feel more exposed than Karin, as if his whole being was splayed out, while she would sit with her knees raised, her crossed arms gracefully covering her breasts.

They would discuss what they were each looking for in life, how everything was spread out in front of them. "Possible, yet impossible," Karin said, drawing back her head.

He told her his parents were philosophy professors, but that because of this or perhaps in opposition to it, he was a realist. He spoke with his hands, making strong jerky movements; he had never felt more earnest.

One rainy afternoon he allowed Karin to photograph him, his nakedness. She was intent and exacting as she instructed him on how to pose.

A few days later, on an unseasonably cool night, they retired early to their room. She sat on the bed reading a photography magazine with a picture of the Taj Mahal on the cover, while he lay on the floor, his back against the rough surface; he held open a book about Florence and the Medici family. He would be heading to Italy in three days, hoping for warmer weather.

Karin suddenly looked up, pushed aside her bangs, and caught his gaze. She spoke directly, dispassionately. "Gregory, what is it that irks you?"

He was startled, but not by her question. What surprised him was the tone of her voice. It touched him, pierced into him as if he were being given a needle by an expert phlebotomist.

He looked at her, forcing his voice to sound as dispassionate as hers, and said, "I do not want to be who I am."

"Not be who you are," she repeated, as if urging him to say more.

He saw she was intrigued.

He continued to speak, fearful that if he stopped, or his tone changed, the mood between them would dissipate.

He told her he had a disease of the temperament—passivity—and explained how he believed he was lost, how he had never really connected with anyone in his life. He was afraid he would simply drift away because that was what happened to people like him. He was moving through life, detached and alone. He had come to Europe to rid himself of this passivity. But nothing had changed. He still was who he was. His temperament was as slow and as uneventful as a waltz.

When he finished speaking, Karin looked at him in that direct way of hers, the night outside growing darker, her face seeming more and more distant. She went to him and caressed his face with her long fingers, cold, assuring. "No. You are not simply moving through life, you have substance, you are my lover," she whispered.

For years he would recall her words, never fully realizing the effect they had had on him at the time or the effect they would have on him in the future.

"I have a temperament problem," he would say, wringing his hands, to each therapist he went to for his usual first and only session, and then he would repeat Karin's words to him or her: "You are my lover." Saying those words was an anodyne, temporarily relieving him of his angst.

On the night before they parted, Karin told Gregory she did not want to separate from him, that she loved him. She spoke in that too-serious way of hers.

Gregory felt angry, not knowing why or when his anger toward her had begun. At first he thought it was because he had revealed so much of himself to her. He was the one who had sat naked on the bed while she had seductively draped her arms round her body. What would she do with those photographs of him? Would they be out there for all to see? Or, when she eventually realized he had no intention of pursuing the relationship, would she fling them out her window? He imagined pictures of his naked self floating in the air before touching ground.

He promised to write and see her again soon, maybe next year. But he knew he would never again contact her. When she wasn't in sight, he had torn up her phone number and address to prove to himself he was serious.

He sensed Karin's melancholy when they parted, as if she knew what he had been thinking, feeling.

A week later, at the Uffizi Gallery in Florence, standing before Botticelli's *Birth of Venus*, he felt a sudden pang for Karin. He was raw inside, as if he had lost part of himself.

He wanted to call her, realizing he had been too rational. But he was unable to reach her. He could not remember the correct spelling of her family name. He tried different spellings. But nobody knew her wherever he called. Perhaps her number was not listed. He hadn't thought she would be difficult to find when he had confidently, justifiably ripped up her name and address. But he had done it with finality; he had not wanted to be able to reach her.

He caught a plane to Frankfurt, then took a train to the small town where they had met, to see if she would reappear. It was in the middle of the afternoon, and the four accordion players were there, playing that hollow-sounding music. Gregory continued to look about the station for Karin. He was young, he kept telling himself; he would survive the pain, the amputation.

III

Gregory Budowski had met Sheila Gerard two months shy of his thirty-third birthday. She was the temporary replacement for the full-time art teacher who was on maternity leave. Each morning he would watch Sheila walk quickly up the front steps of the looming brick building, carrying a canvas bag filled with construction paper and paintbrushes she had purchased for her students. They would both arrive at the same time, earlier than most of the other teachers.

Sheila told him she needed to get to school early because she had to do the lesson planning she should have done the previous day. She could not afford to lose the afternoon light, so she left school soon after the final bell sounded to go to her studio and paint.

Gregory told her he was there at seven thirty to do his lesson planning too. But he did not add that after he left the high school in the early afternoon, he would forget about his work and students and ride the subway into Cambridge, sit in a café; over an espresso he would pretend to read a newspaper or magazine or he would listen in on other people's conversations while contemplating his past failed relationships. With few exceptions, he was unable to clearly recall the features of any women he had known. He could only recreate blurred facial images, like off-center photographs. He would think of his ineptitude, his rash judgments, and then the pain his mistakes had caused others and himself. His blunders were ever present and clear in his mind, in his being; they had become a part of him.

Why had things never turned out quite the way he wanted them to? Each relationship had begun with so much hope. He wasn't certain what love was; he had silently aspired to it, but it had always eluded him.

Sometimes he wondered if he had been trying to punish himself all these years—for what, he wasn't certain—when he thought he had been seeking love.

He would let those thoughts roam about his mind for a moment and then drop them, as if they were reckless, vicious ideas he did not want to admit having because in some way they had given him a sense of comfort, perhaps pleasure. Then he would take a gulp of espresso, warily eyeing the people at the next table, as if they had been privy to his thoughts.

One Friday in late May, Gregory approached Sheila; she was sitting alone in the dark, windowless teachers' room, browsing through an art magazine, sipping coffee from a disposable cup. He shrugged and asked if she would like to go for a drink with him later that afternoon.

Without looking at him, she placed the cup back on the table and said sure, after she finished at the studio.

Gregory picked her up at five o'clock. They drove past worn brick buildings with zigzagging fire escapes, the warm spring air billowing through the open windows. Finally he pulled up in front of a restaurant with a lounge.

He sat across from Sheila in a booth next to a bay window. The bright green leaves of an oak brushed against the glass, heavily shadowing the table and seats. Whenever she inclined her head to the side, or raised her hand to her cheek, he felt as if he were observing her from a distance as she maneuvered through covering shadows.

She didn't say anything after they ordered; she sat there, her hands folded, vaguely smiling, her thoughts elsewhere, he assumed. It struck him how shallow his knowledge of her was. To break the silence he asked her a simple question, an obvious one. Why art? He leaned forward, his gaze meeting her uncertain gray eyes.

Unclasping her hands, she furrowed her brows and told him in a tight, succinct voice that her father had died when she was fourteen. He had worked in a post office, and he had died right there on the job. He was sorting mail when a heavy instrument from a shelf above had fallen on his head. A freak accident, she said.

The spring following his death she had gone with her class to the art museum. She had always liked to draw, but had never been inside an art museum before. She had been feeling sad, depressed, older than her classmates—they all seemed so happy, so free.

When she studied the paintings she saw movement—a woman's gown rustling, the heavy breathing of a man pulling a cart. From that point on, on most Saturday mornings, she would take a bus and then a subway into the city to go to the museum.

Her mother had worked during the day as a bank teller, and every night, after bidding Sheila a stoic good evening, she would shuffle off to bed in her furry gray slippers, holding the latest romance novel she was reading in one hand, and a glass of wine in the other.

Gregory was impressed with Sheila's story and wondered why he had never needed to immerse himself in anything. Though his childhood had not been touched by tragedy as Sheila's had, it had not been a very comforting one. Neither of his parents had been very relaxed in the presence of their two children, and although they were in the same field, they were not particularly compatible. And so they had obsessively thrown themselves into their work, creating a vacuum for him and his older sister. Yet Sheila—she had had such a harsh background, and had transcended her past. Hadn't she?

He responded by saying that maybe they could go to the museum together. He liked Turner.

He would call Sheila every few weeks. Often reticently, sometimes willingly, she would say yes, yes she would like to see him. At first Gregory wanted to be with her because he was hoping some part of her would rub off on him. She savored life more than he did. Lately he had found himself becoming more and more resigned.

One morning in the teachers' room, as he was placing his lunch in the refrigerator, Sheila said, out of the blue, "Gregory, you try too hard!" Startled, he was overcome by her words; he thought the opposite was true—he believed he did not try at all.

He thought she enjoyed visiting the museum with him, asking him his impressions of the paintings, telling him how she felt about what she saw. And he was beginning to understand what she meant when she spoke about seeing movement in a painting. It wasn't as farfetched as he first assumed. It was something he could grasp intellectually, but could not experience visually. "It has to do with both imagination and reality," Sheila explained. "You must use your imagination to see the reality of the painting—the artist's stroke, although it ends on canvas, continues on in the painter's mind, creating a sense of motion."

"A virtual reality," Gregory answered assuredly.

She placed her hands firmly on her hips and said, "No, it has nothing to do with computers," as if computers were the enemy, he thought. But they weren't. They were undeniably the fabric of society. Was she living in the past? he wondered. Was she immune to technology? But that was what had drawn him to her, he acknowledged; she represented the painful, solid past as well as the chaotic present.

IV

It was now mid-August, late in the afternoon. Drowsy from the heat and mug of beer he hastily drank at the museum café an hour before, Gregory lowered himself onto the leather sofa, half watching Sheila; she was moving about her apartment, hoisting open windows. Extending his arms across the back of the sofa, he sank his head into the crinkly fabric, giving her his full groggy attention. It struck him that he had been seeing Sheila for a little over two years, and he frankly did not know her.

All the windows in her third-floor apartment were now open, but there was still no breeze. Tilting his head, he studied her halter dress, how it clung to her, like a loose, moist bandage. As he closed his eyes, his desire for her, thumping and inconsistent, surfaced.

Ice cubes clacking against glass broke the warm silence in the room. He realized she was in the kitchen. She had vanished soundlessly, without leaving a trace, like a ghost.

Now there she was standing in the doorway, each hand clutching a buoying glass of sangria by the stem, sunlight flickering across her form, her mouth open, awed from the heat.

She placed one glass on the oak coffee table, and he watched expectantly as she extended her bare arm, handing him the other glass. As he took it, he felt the wet from her hand.

"Taste it," she said, insistently.

He pressed the glass to his mouth and sipped, gazing up at her.

As Gregory drank, Sheila eased herself downward, sat on the floor, tucked her knees under the table, nestled her pointy elbows against the wooden surface, raised the glass to her lips. They had made love a few weeks before, he thought. Now it seemed so unreal.

Her shoulders dropped forward and she pressed her forehead with the palm of her hand. "I've been hoping to set up a show for the fall," she said directly, "but it's not going very smoothly. This new critic in town has judged my oils harshly. He's awful. My work, he says, is precise and static, more like a waltz than a sonata."

"I like your work, Sheila," Gregory said, hovering over her, waiting for her to lift her head; he focused on wisps of hair swirling at the nape of her neck. "I don't think it's static—it is quite energetic, if you really look at it." But she still refused to look up at him.

He thought about the painting of hers he liked most, the painting of a cracked egg, the background misty, surreal—yes, still, but haunting, discomforting. He found solace in this, in her stillness.

Slightly raising her head, she peered into the hollow of the glass, fingering the rim. Though she had not moved, he felt as if she had walked away from him. And he knew it was time for him to leave.

"More sangria?" she asked. Shadows wobbled across the table; the sun was lowering, the heat relentless.

"No, I have to go," he said.

There was no elevator in the building, so he ambled down the worn marble stairs.

The sky slowly darkening, the heat a formless presence facing him, he strode toward his car, parked three blocks away.

He was angry, very angry that Sheila was holding back from him. He would never see her again, he promised himself. But he knew, despite his anger, this was unrealistic; being with her, watching her stark, hopeful movements, gratified and reassured him.

A Friday afternoon, early September; it was the end of the first week of school. Gregory closed the classroom door behind him. He made his way down the dark, empty corridor. As he went toward the side exit, he came upon two students embracing, jammed in a narrow space between metal lockers—arms, bodies frenetically entwined; he caught a glimpse of the young woman's face, her expression of raw passion, and he was pained. He didn't say anything to them, just kept walking.

As he opened the door, he heard a gasp, and then "Budowski," his name, as if he was the enemy, staid, set in his ways, personally incomplete, beyond understanding what they were experiencing. He felt empty inside, then a deep ache.

The next morning, a Saturday, he woke early. He peered out the kitchen window: brief signs of autumn were beginning to show, trees wavering sporadically from a gust of cool air now and then, a single yellow leaf on an otherwise full, green tree.

He reached inside his pocket for his phone, and pressed Sheila's cell number.

Did she want to go for a ride—enjoy whatever was left of summer? he asked. He was feeling incredibly tired, tired of her, tired of his life.

Sheila suggested he come to her apartment.

When she opened the door, she was holding the cell phone to her ear. Motioning for him to come in, she walked to the other side of the room.

He remained in the doorway, studied her back, how erect

her shoulders were as she haltingly spoke into the phone. She's discouraged today, he thought. He overheard bits and pieces of the conversation, and he realized an exhibit of her work she so desperately hoped to put together would probably not materialize.

"If you don't mind, I'd like to go to the museum," she said, putting her phone down on the coffee table.

"Really?" he asked, avoiding her gaze.

As they climbed the steps into the museum, Sheila told him she first wanted to see Degas.

They walked from room to room, crossing the parquet floors without stopping until they reached the Degas room. He followed her as she moved swiftly toward the painting of a lone dancer.

He stood behind her, waiting while she studied it. He was feeling restless, uncomfortable, confined by the museum—he would rather be outdoors, playing tennis. The museum felt empty, hollow, old, he thought.

She turned toward him. "Gregory," she said, her clear, definite voice piercing him. "I've lost something. I cannot see the movement anymore."

Then she reached up and drew her arms round his neck.

Uneasy, he wondered if she had not been honest with him. He placed his hands on her arms and took a slight step backward, hoping to slip away from her embrace. Not knowing where to look, his eyes fastened on the painting of the Degas dancer. The dancer's extended arm formed a semicircle and as Gregory watched he imagined it rising, as if to stop him. His gaze locked on the painting, he could not move; it was as if it were all those years ago and he was sitting in that north German train station, looking up at the musicians on the platform.

He recalled the hollow-sounding music, and how on the surface he had been uncertain, anxious, every so often he had glanced around, his eyes straining for Karin, hoping to catch a glimpse of her haunted but kind expression. Though within he had begun to grow calm, expectant; he thought he had taken a step forward by returning to that spot, searching for her, fully believing his life in some way was only beginning.